Digging the Driver

Celebrity Corgi Romance

Elsie Davis

Sweet Romance Publishing

Many thanks to all my readers.
May love and laughter light your path always...

John 8:32

And you will know the truth, and the truth will set you free.

Chapter One

♥

"Now turn toward me, hands on your hips. That's it. A gentle smile. Now tip your head back just a little more. Perfect. Let your hair cascade down your back. Look right at the camera. Perfect."

Lissa did as she was instructed, but only because she'd learned long ago just to cooperate. It was the easiest way to get these photo sessions over with and the hordes of people surrounding her to vanish.

"One last shot, and we can call it quits. Left hand up over your head and angled back down. Turn your right shoulder inward a little more. Let's see you flirt a little with the camera, like you would with a new man in your life."

New man? It was the last thing she wanted. The only thing she needed was her sweet corgi, Bella. Now that was a relationship she could trust.

Images of Bella at the rescue shelter looking lost and afraid still had the power to make Lissa's heart ache. Poor thing must have been the runt of the litter because she was small for a corgi. Add to that not being fed very well, and she'd been downright bony. It had been a spur-of-the-moment decision to get a pet of her own finally.

Growing up, she'd often visited the shelter in Bellevue, a small bedroom community just outside of Charlotte, and had helped out whenever she could. Every animal in the place deserved a loving home. It broke her heart each time she'd left, their sad and confused faces calling to her to do something more for them.

Adopting Bella was the smartest decision she ever made. Lissa had gone looking for a pet, but what she'd found was much better. She'd found a best friend. It was also the day she started working at the rescue shelter regularly, hoping to make a difference for so many other animals who deserved more than to be homeless.

She hadn't seen the direction her help would take at the time, but she was pleased with the inroads of success being made over the past four years.

Bloom magazine, stopped taking pictures, her mouth in a tight line. "Remember, this is *La Bella*, your signature scent. A scent that empowers women to not only feel beautiful but to take on the world with power and confidence. A scent to inspire woman to greater heights."

"Sorry. I'm a little tired." *Tired of being photographed*—one of the top three things she hated about her celebrity driver status.

"Okay, try this. Imagine you're looking at a new stock car just delivered, and you're ready to slide into the driver's seat and test out the way it handles on the racetrack for the first time."

A sweet image for sure. The clicking whirr of the camera was a good sign.

Thank goodness.

"Sorry, Emily. Sometimes, it's hard to get into the right frame of mind for something like this."

"No worries. Trust me, I get all kinds of scenarios when it comes to bringing out the best in my subjects. You're one of the easy ones." Emily laughed.

"That's good to hear. Will you be coming to the Walker Charity Gala on June 1st?"

"I'm going to try and make it, but I have some scheduling conflicts. I heard Ruby Ross and some of the others from *Bloom* magazine will be there."

"Yes. It'll be great to see Ruby again," Lissa said, excited at the prospect of seeing her friend again.

"You two knew each other before the *Bloom* connection, didn't you?"

"We met in college, but we didn't actually connect back then." Ruby was one of those women that surprised you once you got to know them. Or maybe the problem was Lissa's. Unfortunately, she hadn't given the woman a chance back then.

"Funny how life brings people back into your life for a second chance." Emily laughed, tucking her camera into the hard-shell case.

"True." Ruby was a powerhouse in the fashion industry, and they had become friends at the extravagant parties *Bloom* threw each year.

Lissa had been honored to be invited to attend Ruby's recent wedding to Brandon Price, one of the sexiest men alive according to People's Magazine Sexiest 25. The reception party had been touted in every magazine for months and was easily considered the "in" wedding of the year. Marriage wasn't in the cards for Lissa, but it was nice to see those around her happy.

"It looks like everyone's almost got everything cleaned up in here. I should probably get a move on. It was great to see you again."

"You, too." Lissa watched as Emily followed the rest of her crew down the hall to leave.

Bev, her friend and marketing manager, and one of the few people she truly trusted, was deep in conversation with one of the set assistants. During the photoshoot, Bev had stood on the sidelines with Bella, watching the progress.

She'd met Bev Masters when she'd first come onto the racing scene five years ago, and they'd become friends. Bev was in marketing, and when she'd gotten wind Lissa had entered the pole event for what is considered the longest and most grueling stock car race at the Charlotte Motor Speedway, she'd gone out of her way to contrive a meeting. It wasn't often a woman took on the challenge of the racing against the biggest names in the business, especially for her debut race. It had taken a bit of fancy footwork on Bev's part, but in the end, Lissa was glad she'd given the woman a chance to prove herself.

The celebrity endorsements that came with competing in a man's world required a full-time person to manage. Over time, Bev had earned her trust—something Lissa didn't give out easily. After her parents' success in the video world, she'd learned the hard way that trust wasn't a five-letter word, it was four. L-I-E-S.

Bev was different from the other people who wanted her attention, and now Lissa wasn't sure what she would do without her. The picture of smooth efficiency, the woman always looked like she'd stepped straight out of a magazine with everything effortlessly in place, unlike the hours it took Lissa to transform herself from her usual never-ready harried look. Her friend understood her better than anyone, including her need to race cars.

Racing was the ultimate in control, something Lissa craved after having spent years on the sidelines at first by choice, and then later as the result of her parents' video gaming success catapulting her into a world she didn't understand. A world where people thought nothing of using someone to get what they wanted. A world she hated.

The crew soon left, and finally, the house was back to the peace and quiet Lissa enjoyed.

"I'm glad that's over." Lissa glanced at her watch. "Travis Howard from SDS should be here soon for our appointment." Yet another interruption to her solitude, but this one had a more far-reaching impact.

"Thank goodness." Bev offered her a light cardigan.

Lissa slid it over her bare shoulders to cover the satiny material of the halter top that left her chilled. The top had been the art director at *Bloom* magazine's choice for Lissa's signature fragrance advertisement. Neither Lissa nor Bev had control when it came to these photo shoots if they stayed within the preset guidelines—nothing scanty or provocative.

She wasn't exactly model material, and her well-developed, muscular arms and solidly built frame were accentuated instead of hidden. Something she'd tried to do most of her life. Lissa had learned first-hand how catty and mean people could be from jealousy, wanting what she had and not understanding how hard she worked to get where she was on the racing circuit.

"We've talked about this and I'm sorry. But there's a lot going on the next few weeks, and I can't always babysit Bella. Not that I mind, you understand, it's just sometimes it makes my job impossible." Bev handed Bella to Lissa.

Bella bombed her face with doggie kisses from a wet tongue, and Lissa rubbed her cheek dry.

Her baby was spoiled but too darn cute to resist. Bella had the airs and grace of a princess, and over the years, she'd insisted on being treated like one. When Lissa had first brought her home, she'd barely weighed in at ten pounds and carrying her around had been easy, but at twenty-two pounds now, it was a different story. Lissa didn't have the heart to say no when she yipped to be held, and truth be told, she enjoyed being needed by her canine companion.

"I understand. It stinks we even need to worry about a dognapper, but yesterday's dognapping makes eleven in the Charlotte vicinity. The dogs are all purebreds, but there have been no ransom notes yet. I can't stand the thought of Bella being taken by these unsavory characters for who knows what purpose."

Lissa had been toying with the idea of security for Bella because she wasn't always in a position to keep her safe. Yesterday's incident was the final straw that prompted the call to South Division Securities. SDS came highly recommended, and when she found out Travis Williams worked there, it had been a no-brainer to use the company.

The only downside being that he was her former best friend's cousin. The three of them had been close back in high school, at least they were until her world had been turned upside down by her parents' success. She'd always wondered what happened to Damien, but it was easier not to think of him or the way he'd hurt her. Travis on the other hand, was still a friend, one she ran into occasionally in town. He would be a hundred times better than dealing with a stranger, especially considering he would temporarily be living in her home.

"I know. I just wish the police would catch these criminals and put an end to the fear these dognappings have created in everyone's hearts. I can't even begin to imagine what these pet owners feel having their babies stolen."

Lissa snuggled Bella close and kissed the top of her head. "The photographers are gone, baby girl. And don't you worry, Mommy's going to keep you safe from those bad guys." She sat down on the sofa and leaned back; Bella happily situated against her chest.

"Bella's not a real baby, you know." Bev laughed.

"She is to me." Lissa nuzzled up against Bella's cheek, loving the feel of her silky fur if you brushed it in the right direction.

"Technically, she's forty-two years old in people years." Bev moved to the side table and poured herself a glass of wine. "Want one?" She nodded her head to indicate the wine.

"Sure. It might help relax me for this next appointment. Forty-two or otherwise, what dog doesn't love to be pampered?" Lissa smiled. She put Bella down on the floor and accepted the glass of wine, eager for a moment to relax. Bella took off down the hall, probably in search of one of her toys.

"Bella has you wrapped."

"Probably, but I like it. You know, I've mentioned it before, but I'd like to start doing less and less of these endorsements. They're just not me." She took a sip of wine, enjoying the crisp sauvignon blanc.

"They may not be you, but they are part of your image. An image that pays bank when it comes to marketing. You're living in a man's world, and there's big money in the fact that you're all woman. Something I'm sure none of the male drivers can forget."

"Which isn't necessarily a good thing. Some of them can be downright insulting, their egos are not quite up to a little feminine competition."

"True." Bev smiled. "I'll see what I can do to cut back on your commitments, but we need to get through the ones scheduled already. Things are ramped up right now with the second annual Walker Rescue Shelter Gala coming up. You know, the one you personally endorse."

"I hear you. And for the rescue dogs, I'll put up with anything, but then you already knew that."

"I do. Don't forget we need to be at the Taylors' pre-gala cocktail party by seven-thirty tonight. There will be some big names, and hopefully some big donations. The Taylors are counting on you."

Lissa let out a frustrated sigh. It would have been nice just relax the rest of the evening, considering she had practice time scheduled on the track in the morning. Traveling at speeds of over two hundred miles per hour was dangerous, doing it at less than one hundred percent focus could be deadly.

"I'll be ready." Somehow, she'd have to get through the party and get a good night's sleep, something made even less likely with Travis sleeping under her roof for the near future. It would take some getting used to the idea of having a security detail around twenty-four-seven for Bella.

Chapter Two

♥

DAMIEN TURNED ONTO SUNSET River Way, shaking his head at the showy estates in the gated community, each one grandiose in its own way. These people had plenty of the almighty dollar, but no kids were playing in the yard, no toys left out haphazardly, or animals running loose. Instead, everything here was coldly impersonal and meticulously cared for. The old adage about money not buying happiness came to mind.

Of course, this is where Lissa Walker lived. He'd expected nothing less from the famous Walkers and their spoiled daughter. He was, however, surprised she'd even stayed in Bellevue. He'd pegged her and Tony Carruthers as two people this little town could never satisfy. Of course, it was no more surprising than when he'd found out she was competing on a professional level at the Charlotte Motor Speedway in the Coca-Cola 600.

On the other hand, Tony, Bellevue High's superstar, super stud, and super jerk, had left right after high school to play college football. He'd never made it as a professional player, which didn't hurt Damien's feelings one bit.

Damien used to enjoy football and racing, but between Lissa and Tony, they'd manage to ruin both sports for him. Mr. King and Queen of the senior prom were welcome to whatever they got in life. Damien was just glad he'd discovered the real Lissa Walker before he'd spilled his guts to her about his feelings.

He pulled into the driveway and entered the gate code his cousin had given him. Travis had a legitimate reason he couldn't be at the appointment he'd scheduled. Damien, on the other hand, had a legitimate reason *not* to want to be here. *Lissa.*

Damien shook his head as he surveyed the manicured lawn and bushes. It was late spring, and most lawns were just starting to turn green, but hers, like every other house in this neighborhood, were bright green and would have been for months. Overseeded with rye, most likely by a professional gardener. Nothing but the best for a Walker.

The house, correction, make that the mansion—was built of stone and stood three stories high. The widow's walk at the top would provide an unparalleled view of the Catawba River and the countryside.

He'd give anything to be back at the office reviewing his most recent client's corporate files. Figuring out who was hacking into their computers was far more appealing than covering for his cousin, but family was important to him.

Saying no to Travis was never really a choice, not after what his family had done for Damien's family. Travis's mother had them all move in and helped his family weather through the worst of times after the media storm that ruined Damien's parents' lives. A storm filled with sensationalism and lies, but no one cared when the truth finally came out—by then it was old news.

All except for the family they destroyed in the process.

Damien slid out of the jeep and made his way to the porch. A little tan, white, and black dog came through the open front door and started to bark. Damien chuckled, hoping the dog had more bark than bite. It was a funny-looking, squatty thing with the shortest legs he'd ever seen on a dog.

He looked around but didn't see anyone nearby. The dog continued to bark, doing a miniature show of charge and retreat, as if unsure how brave he wanted to be. Damien knelt to let the cute little fellow smell his hand. The dog inched his way closer and the barking stopped.

Damien stroked his back lightly. "Hey there, little guy. What are you doing out here?"

The dog couldn't answer, of course, but talking was all Damien could think of to do to calm the dog enough so that he could pick him up and take him back inside. It's not like he wanted to get his hand bit off in the process. Damien's experience with dogs amounted to zero, but leaving the dog outside wasn't an option, just in case he had escaped.

Damien picked up the dog, more than a little surprised when the dog didn't seem to mind. He stepped up on the porch and knocked, pushing the door open further at the same time. He took one tentative step inside, glancing down the hall. "Hello? Anyone home?" He spotted someone coming toward him.

"Hey there, who are you? That's my dog! Put her down!"

Lissa Walker in the flesh.

The suddenness of coming face-to-face with her slowed the function of his brain and his ability to respond.

"Bev, call the police!" Lissa hollered.

Police? "Whoa! Hold up a minute." He held up his free hand. "There's no need for the police. Your front door was open, and I did knock. Your dog was outside. I thought I was doing you a favor by bringing him back inside to keep him from running away." So much for being cool and reserved. He'd never had the police called on him before, and he didn't intend to start now.

"Damien?" The word was filled with derision, and her face scrunched up as if his name tasted like bile.

It's not like he had expected a warm welcome, but this was over the top. He handed Bella to Lissa. "It's nice to know you remember me." Especially since he hadn't forgotten her—not that he hadn't tried. But with her face plastered on every racing magazine, not to mention several others that lined the shelves at the grocery store checkouts, it wasn't like he could forget.

Seeing her in magazines had done nothing to prepare him for the up-close-and-personal view he had now. Beautiful, poised, and in control. Her sapphire-blue eyes were filled with icy scorn. Her dark-brown hair, once short and fluffy, fell in long gorgeous tresses across her shoulders. An urge to smooth back the loose tendrils from her cheek threatened to overwhelm him, but he held it in check. He despised the male appreciation he couldn't seem to control.

"Thank you." The words seemed dragged from her lips. "For your information, the photoshoot crew just left, and they must have left the door open. It's not an invitation to walk into someone's home. What are you doing here?"

"I'm with SDS. Travis had a family emergency and asked me to fill in for him. I understand you need security."

"I do. Or I did. Not with you." She stood feet apart, one hand clutching the dog, the other wrapped protectively around the animal as she rubbed behind her ears.

"Suit yourself. I wasn't keen on this job myself." At least there was one thing they could agree upon. Damien turned to leave.

"Wait a minute. What's going on here?" Another voice made Damien hesitate and turn back.

A woman had joined them, pushing her glasses back on her nose to get a better look. She was the epitome of efficiency, and her tone demanded answers.

"He's with SDS. Travis can't make it and thought it would be okay to send Damien. It's not. Okay, that is." Lissa huffed.

"Damien?" The woman looked him over from head to toe, the look of appreciation in her eyes all too obvious.

"Damien Trent, to be exact. An old, let's say, ex-friend, from high school."

The woman looked back and forth between him and Lissa. She shook her head. "What does it matter who provides the security? What matters is that you have it. You know how important it is, Lissa."

"I am standing here, ladies. So, what's it going to be? Do you need a bodyguard or not? Or is this just another celebrity ploy to show off your popularity and wealth?"

Damien didn't like the sudden smirk that turned Lissa's thin-lined lips upward ever so slightly. The feeling of unease grew when she shot the other woman a quick look and shook her head. Secret code for don't say a word. He'd seen the look time and time again in his business, and it was never good.

"I do need security. You say you're filling in for Travis?" Her grinned widened.

"I am. Just for a few days." Lissa was up to no good. One minute she was ready to call the police, and the next she seemed all too happy to let him take over Travis's contract.

"Travis signed on for full-time. Our deal was for him to stay on for as long as I felt extra security was needed. Are you prepared for that?" The dog nudged her hand to continue the rubbing when Lissa stopped.

"That's fine. Is there any reason you've suddenly become gung-ho for security that I should know about? Travis didn't provide me with very many details. I thought I could get those from you." The truth was Damien hadn't given his cousin much chance to explain once he'd found out the name of the client.

"There have been no threats if that's what you're asking. I just want precautionary security."

"It's always been about you, hasn't it? At least it has been ever since your parents came out with their Dark Dragon Hunter videogame." The sarcasm in his voice couldn't be helped. Not after all these years.

"You have no idea what you're talking about. But back in high school, you didn't stick around long enough to find out. Let's just hope when the going gets tough working for me, you don't run away again." She bit down on the side of her lower lip as if to keep from saying anything else. If she bit it any harder, she'd soon draw blood.

"I'm only here until Travis can take over his own assignment. There's not much I can't handle, so don't worry. I've got you covered. The contract terms call for the arrangement to start in the morning and I'll be here first thing." At least it would give him the night to readjust to what the next few days would be like because seeing her in person was a whole lot harder than dealing with the memory.

"What? Travis knew I had a cocktail party to attend tonight. We talked about it and he agreed to cover for me."

"She's right. He did agree. Surely you can cancel your plans for the evening. This is important to Lissa." The woman was quick to jump in and try to help sway his decision. Two against one but it wouldn't work.

"Travis said nothing about starting tonight and I have a prior engagement. This was supposed to be just a precursor meeting to iron out some of the details. Sorry ladies, but I really can't stay." Damien nodded his head and turned to leave.

"But what am I supposed to do with Bella?" Lissa spoke up, stopping him as he reached for the doorknob.

He glanced back. "Bella?"

Lissa started down the hall toward him. "My dog." She pointed at the corgi still safely ensconced in her arms.

"How should I know? I'm not a dog person, but I would think whatever you normally do with her."

"That's why I hired SDS. I can't do what I normally do, not with the dognappers still on the loose."

"What does SDS have to do with Bella?" Damien was totally confused at this point, but an uneasy feeling settled in the pit of his stomach.

"You're her guard. You know, your job. Bella's new doggy guard." Her words sunk in like a kick to the solar plexus.

"I agreed to nothing of the sort. Travis indicated you needed security, a bodyguard. I'm not babysitting a dog. Check her into doggy daycare or something like that—like normal people do. Have a good evening, ladies."

The sparkle in Lissa's eyes was a telltale sign she'd known he didn't have a clue as to the true purpose of why SDS had been hired, and she'd enjoyed dropping the bomb. It explained the secret the two women had shared earlier. He shouldn't have expected anything less from Lissa, but it didn't change anything. He wasn't babysitting a dog.

"So you're running away? Again. You haven't changed much, have you? How will it look for SDS when you renege on a contract? Because you can be sure everyone will find out. Bella needs protection, and the way I see it, you don't have a choice. Unless Travis has some other underling, one he can force to take his place for a few days. Bella means everything to me, and that means putting up with having security people around, even if it's you." Her threat landed its mark.

Backed into a corner, he didn't have much choice. "Fine. First thing in the morning, I'll be here. Seven a.m. sharp. It's only for a couple of days. And for the record, the dislike you have for me, it's mutual. It'll make things easier with us being on the same page."

Chapter Three

♥

A DOGGY GUARD. DAMIEN shook his head, unable to believe Lissa had trapped him into saying yes. Although technically, SDS had a reputation to protect and with Travis having agreed to work with Lissa as a client, the company was honor bound to fulfill the contract. But it didn't mean he had to like it.

Damien slammed the door of his Jeep a little harder than necessary and punched in the speed-dial number for Travis as he put the truck in drive.

"Hey there. Everything okay? How did your appointment go?" Travis knew why he was calling, the hesitation in his voice a dead giveaway.

"You know exactly how it went. You tricked me into taking this job. It was bad enough this was for Lissa Walker, but Lissa Walker's dog? You knew I would've said no if you'd told me the truth." Damien glanced down at the speedometer and eased off the accelerator. Angry driving wouldn't solve anything.

"You're right, I did. But seriously, how bad can it be? It's just a little dog. Besides, you owe me."

"You're not referring to the Marilyn Malloy incident, are you? It wasn't that big of a deal." That was a topic best left alone.

"If you don't consider getting caught in a bedroom with a married woman by her husband a big deal, then you're right. We both know she set you up, but her husband wouldn't have believed you if I hadn't shown up in the nick of time to make everything look legit."

Damien didn't want to think about Marilyn and how close he'd come to falling prey to one of the oldest tricks in the books. He was a nice guy and had made it altogether too easy for Marilyn when he agreed to help hang a new painting. It had been too late to say no when he found out she wanted it hung in one of the bedrooms.

Being the nice guy always meant finishing last. Just like it had with Lissa.

"Yeah, yeah. But still, you could've told me. Lissa took great joy in being the one to explain my mistake and my responsibility. I don't know a thing about dogs, and now I get to babysit one. I'll be the laughingstock at the office if they get word of this, so try not to run your mouth. I expect you here, taking over doggie duty in a few days—or else."

"Or else what?" Travis chuckled, not in the least afraid of Damien. It reminded him of Bella—more bark than bite.

"Forget it. You are family, and you know there is no *or else*. Just get back to Bellevue in a couple of days. I'm not sure I can deal with Lissa for much longer than that." Damien turned onto the highway and headed for Beeson Park.

"You two used to be friends. Best friends, I might add."

"You're right. And then came her parents' overnight multimillion-dollar video game success. And in the same space of time, the shy quiet girl I was friends with became Miss Popularity and started dating the quarterback. I prefer real people, not shallow socialites in action. And trust me, she's not any different now. Still spoiled and with too much time and money on her hands."

And still beautiful.

Once upon a time, he'd thought of her like a shrinking violet—timid, yet lovely. Seeing her today made him think of the bleeding hearts that once grew in his mother's garden. Showy flowers that captured one's attention with the intricately shaped heart, but upon closer inspection, revealed what looked like tears or blood dripping from the bottom. It was a flower his mother considered romantic, but Damien thought it was quite the opposite, representing the hurt love could inflict on people.

"Strong reaction for a guy who doesn't care. You sure you don't still have feelings for her?" Travis had it all wrong. For a second, he considered sharing his bleeding heart funny, but Lissa was still a client, and it would cross the lines of professionalism.

"Hardly. I prefer the quieter side of life and people you can trust."

"Well then, I hate to have to tell you this, but things have changed on my end. The surgery didn't go as well as expected, and the doctor said I should plan on sticking around for at least another week or two, depending on how quickly mother improves. There's nothing I can do about it, because no one else is in a position to drop everything and come sit with her twenty-four-seven, and she can't be left alone."

Damien gripped the wheel harder. "And how am I supposed to manage taking care of Lissa's dog and everything else at the office?"

"Sorry. Just work from the house—her house, that is. You can make it work if you want to. Besides, Lissa's easy on the eye, and it could be fun to get reacquainted with the Maneater. I hear she doesn't let many people get close to her. It's a great opportunity. Think of the publicity." It wasn't a very complimentary nickname, but it certainly fit Lissa's hard-core personality.

"I'm not interested in getting reacquainted or in the publicity. Both are great reasons why I should say no to this ridiculous request of yours. Why did you even agree to take her on as a client in the first place?"

"Because she sounded worried, and that's what we do, right? Help people who need us. Besides, we were all friends once upon a time. I don't recall anything in the employee manual that says no doggy guard cases. Say you'll do it. If not for me, then do it for my mother."

Damien exited the highway and stopped at the top of the ramp to wait for the light.

"Fine. Aunt Beth has always been good to us. It's the least I can do. But two weeks tops, and if you're not back, you need to find someone else to pick up the slack. I told her I'd start in the morning." Damien shook his head, finding it hard to believe he'd just agreed to babysit a dog for two weeks. He must be out of his mind to think this would end well.

"But I promised her I'd be there tonight. She has some party to go to."

"Something else you failed to mention, and not my problem. I have plans, and I have no intention of canceling them."

"So, who's the lucky lady tonight?" Travis pressed for more information with good reason.

Damien didn't date often, even less since the Marilyn incident as his cousin like to call the debacle.

"No one you know."

It was more like fourteen dates and a baseball diamond that would capture his interest. Damien smiled. His Little League team had come a long way since the start of the season, and he'd grown to care for the boys, watching them gain confidence and become a team.

Lissa hadn't been prepared to face off with Damien. Not now. Not ever. It didn't help that he looked so darn good. The young man who once had the young girls in high school swooning for his attention had matured, and his dark hair and brown eyes were an even more powerful combination with the five o'clock shadow he sported now. Tall and muscular, his T-shirt and jeans displayed his athletic build. When he had first stepped into the hall, the sunlight behind him had blinded her, but once he'd spoken, she had quickly recognized his voice.

She didn't like it when things happened that she couldn't control, which is why she loved racing. She was in control of her destiny, at least until some lunatic driver tried to get in her way or bump her. Damien was just like those guys on the racetrack. Unable to handle a woman competing with them at their own level.

"Bev, I know what I said to Damien, but you really need to cancel any appointments I have until Travis gets back and takes over. I'll go tonight, but Bella goes with me, whether they like it or not. There's no way I can trust Damien to watch Bella. He said it himself, he doesn't know a thing about dogs. And I know enough about him to make me worry." She took a sip of wine, hoping to calm her nerves.

It was one thing to force herself to trust someone like Travis in her home, but Damien was another story. She'd goaded him into upholding the SDS contract but seeing it through on her end would be lunacy. Sleep would be impossible knowing he was in her home, in a bed just down the hall.

"I'm sorry, Lissa. We just can't at this point. There's only tonight's party, your practice track time tomorrow, and then a press conference and luncheon the day after. There's nothing the next day, and by then Travis will take over. Surely you both can handle this for a couple of days. People are counting on you." Bev glanced up from her phone long enough to level Lissa with a direct, don't-argue-with-me gaze. Her friend didn't use it often.

"I wish we could count on SDS. Damien's prob- ably out on a date. Heaven forbid he cancel to help us out." Men like Damien didn't need money to attract women, his good looks would win hearts every time. It was just one other reason to resent him.

"Spoken by the woman who doesn't date. This guy really has you bent out of shape."

"Not this time. He may have been able to rattle me in high school when I was young and naïve, but I'm not the same girl I was back then. We used to be good friends, or so I thought. And then suddenly, he ditched me, and I never understood why." *Good riddance.*

"Maybe he'll surprise you and be different now." Bev laughed as she picked up her briefcase and grabbed her keys off the table.

"No. He must be getting something out of this deal. A promotion. Publicity for SDS. I don't know, but I'm sure we'll eventually find out. I just hope I don't regret letting him stay here."

"You're too cynical." Bev shook her head.

"Maybe so. But everybody wants something. I learned that the hard way, and Damien...well, he was just the first in a long line of many to prove me right."

"Don't be late tonight. I'm sure the Taylors won't mind you bringing Bella, and I'll help with her when I can. It's just one more night to make it work."

Bev left, and as if sensing Lissa was distressed, Bella jumped in her lap and gave her a doggy kiss. Lissa stroked her back and under her belly, enjoying the close connection they shared.

"He's an insufferable man, and I'm sorry, but I'm going to have to let him take care of you when I'm busy." A little scratch behind the ears for good measure earned Lissa another doggy kiss. "I'll make it up to you, I promise." Bella barked in agreement.

An hour later, dressed and ready, Lissa pulled out of the garage. She put the Porsche in drive, loving the power packed under the hood. It wasn't as much as her stock car, but it was a close second. Bella stood with her paws against the passenger door to look out the window, happy not to have been left at home. A rare occurrence, but one that in the past had sometimes been unavoidable. But now, with dognappers on the loose, there was no way she'd leave her alone. Not even for a minute.

She pulled up to the Windsor Hotel and handed the valet the keys. "Take good care of Mabel. She's a sweet ride but sensitive." Lissa smiled at the young man who looked starstruck.

"Y-y-yes, Miss Walker. Have a nice evening." It was always this way wherever she went. People recognized her.

Privacy was a thing of the past and had been since her parents became famous. Of course, now, the publicity was all on her. Being a woman and winning at the Charlotte Motor Speedway early in her career, she'd captured the interest of millions.

Her continued success had won their hearts. Fans had rooted her on to win the Superbowl of racing at the Daytona 500. All except the other men who'd raced against her that is. They were the ones who'd dubbed her the Maneater.

So far, a win at Daytona had eluded her, this year no exception. It had been another disappointing loss, but then lots of great names never managed to secure the title. Being a great driver didn't stop and start at Daytona. Racing careers consisted of disappointing losses with a few hard-earned wins scattered in the mix. She'd been lucky enough to have a few in the win column, and it was exciting knowing she was competing with the best of the best. The Charlotte Speedway, however, would always be her hometown favorite and the win had a special place in her heart.

Lissa walked around the car and put Bella in the special bag she had that made it easier to carry her. Bella loved the attention and settled in against her blankets, her head hanging over the edge so as not to miss a thing.

Photographers snapped pictures as guests arrived, their flurry of excitement increasing when they spotted her. Lissa picked up the pace, grateful she didn't trip on the steps in her high heels. That would have given them something to talk about, for sure.

Once inside, the chaos dwindled. She found and entered the ballroom, scanning the room to find their hosts. The chandeliers cast glittering lights to brighten the room. Women dressed in designer dresses and men sporting tuxedos graced the room as they chatted and laughed and danced to the jazz music that was softly playing in the background.

She spotted Jim and Meredith Taylor across the room and made her way to their side after stopping for a glass of wine. They were huge fans of hers, and their pledge to help the rescue-shelter cause was a huge blessing.

"It's lovely to see you. And you even brought Bella to see me." Meredith reached out to pet Bella.

"Beautiful party. Everyone appears to be having a good time. I hope you don't mind that I brought her?"

"Of course not. She's always so well-behaved."

Their conversation was cut short when another guest sought out Meredith's attention. "If you will excuse me, dear. Have fun. And later, you can make your announcement about the charity event."

"Sounds great. And thank you so much for all you do to help the cause."

"My pleasure."

Meredith moved off, and Lissa used the opportunity to talk to others, giving in graciously to those who wanted her to pose for a photograph with them. She noticed Bev across the room and waved as she started her way.

A man stepped in front of her and stopped.

"Well, well. If it isn't the Maneater. I heard you'd be here." Jim Trevor, otherwise known as Razor on the racing circuit, blocked her path.

"And? The Taylors are close friends of mine. What's your point?" Razor was no friend of hers, and someone she typically avoided. Not all the guys were complete jerks, but this one took high honors.

"I'd have thought you'd be at the track practicing. You're going to need it for the 600. You've been lucky so far, but your luck is about to run out. Me and the others are gonna stop treating you like a lady out on the track, cause of course, we know you're not one. You may fool your fans, but those of us who know how to drive...well, we know the truth." The man's breath smelled like whiskey.

She stepped back. "I don't know what your problem is, but I don't have time for this or you. Go climb back into the cockpit of your inferior car and work out your issues on your own time." Lissa started to walk away but Razor's hand caught her arm.

"You're my problem. You don't belong out there," he snarled.

Bella growled. "My track time and record say I do. Get your hand off me before I let Bella take a bite."

Razor pulled his hand back, a surly look on his face. "We'll see about that, Maneater."

Lissa sidestepped him and made her way to Bev's side. "Nice party." She smiled at her friend.

"What was that all about?" Bev had obviously seen the interchange and wanted answers.

"I'm not sure. Trying to get into my head before the race maybe. Not sure who he knows to get invited here, but he was a total jerk. Nothing new, and nothing I can't handle, but I get tired of the slimeball. Maybe if he won occasionally, he'd leave me alone." She laughed.

"Forget him. It's almost time for you to make your announcement." Bev reached out to pet Bella. "How's our little girl doing tonight?"

"Loving the attention." Lissa laughed.

"Of course. Unlike her mother."

"You got that right." Lissa grinned. "Bella just doesn't like the Razor kind of attention. Good thing he didn't know her growl is worse than her bite. Imagine him being afraid of a little corgi."

"Serves him right." Bev grinned, scratching behind Bella's ears. "Good girl."

Lissa had a surprise in store for tonight that even Bev didn't know about. After the announcement about the upcoming Walker Rescue Gala, she'd decided to up the ante by offering passes to significant contributors for the Coca-Cola 600 race next week.

Pit passes were always a winning move when it came to race fans.

Chapter Four

♥

DAMIEN DROVE DOWN THE interstate, the all-too-familiar Lissa Walker billboard a reminder of everything he tried to forget. Larger than life, propped up against her car, hair blowing in the breeze. The camera loved her. Not many women could rock a racing jumpsuit and make it look desirable.

But then Lissa did everything well. She was a symbol of equality, and one of the forerunners of women who'd dared enter a man's world. On the one hand, he was proud of her accomplishments. On the other, her fame symbolized everything he despised, starting with her parents' instant rise to success.

Daddy's little girl had embraced her newfound popularity like a princess holding court over her subjects. A princess that had become a beautiful queen, reigning over her adoring racing fans.

A world he wanted no part of. He'd had enough of that to last a lifetime.

Thinking of the times they'd shared as kids brought back a flood of memories. Damien had been big into racing, and Lissa had become interested in watching it with him.

She'd always said she would race one day, and her dream had become a reality. But at the same time, Damien had lost interest in the races. Once her name and face became a fixture on the circuit, it was too much of a constant reminder of the girl she'd become her senior year. From wallflower to prom queen. Not a change he'd liked.

Damien drove down the now familiar street of posh homes, turned into Lissa's gated drive, and punched in the code. His priority after he got settled in would be to check out her current security. He was only one person and making sure there were cameras to monitor all activity from one spot was crucial. Damien might not like the babysitting job, but while the case was assigned to him, it would be done right.

He knocked on the front door and was completely surprised when Lissa answered. He'd expected an employee to handle such an ordinary chore. Dressed in blue jeans and a tight blue cotton shirt, she looked good. Comfortable. With her hair pulled back in a ponytail, he noticed there weren't any fancy earrings or necklaces to accent her slender neck. Bella looked quite comfortable tucked in her arms.

"Good morning."

"Same to you. Glad to see you could make it."

Not overly welcoming in the least, but fully expected. Their mutual dislike wouldn't simply vanish. The trick would be to figure out how to work together for the short time necessary. "Did someone get up on the wrong side of the bed this morning? Of course, I made it. I said I would." He smiled to make sure she understood he was teasing. The success of their business relationship depended on it.

"No, I didn't wake up wrong. For your information, I'm in a good mood. I'm always in a good mood on track days."

"If this a good mood, I'd hate to see a bad one." She loved racing, so her sour expression must be directly related to his presence.

"Yes. You would. So don't cross me, and all will be fantastic."

Damien silently counted to three before answering. His patience would be sorely tested before this assignment was over. "I need to know your itinerary. Mind if I come in, or do you keep your guests standing on the front porch all day?" It was easier to ignore her comment.

"You're not a guest. You're hired help. Come in. I know neither of us is happy about the situation, so why don't we cut through the bull and establish boundaries and rules."

"Fine by me. Would you prefer I use the back door?" He couldn't help the dig that slipped out. No subtle niceties for the famous Lissa Walker.

Her lips pursed harder if possible as she shook her head, then turned and started down the hall, leaving Damien to follow. The living room was more like a great room, based on the size of it.

Two black leather sofas and an armchair were grouped together with an oversize glass and chrome coffee table as a centerpiece. Racing magazines were the only things scattered across the surface, the disarray at odds with the rest of the room, which appeared starchily perfect. The stone fireplace was massive, the hearth filled with racing trophies. On the walls, framed racing posters featuring the number seventeen car and driver hung proudly.

Lissa set Bella down on the sofa. "Do you need coffee or water before we get started." Businesslike to a T.

"No, thanks." He was thirsty, but he'd get his own drink *after* they'd finished. Damien dropped his duffle bag next to the armchair and sat, choosing a location well away from where Lissa stood, and Bella lay watching him from behind half-closed eyelids. He took a pen and pad of paper from his briefcase and then settled in against the back of the chair.

"Here's where we stand so far. You hired Travis as security for your dog, something he failed to disclose. We work as a team at SDS, and I'm honoring my agreement to fill in, which just to be clear, has been changed from a few days to a couple of weeks."

"Whoa. Stop right there. What do you mean? That's ridiculous."

"We agree on one thing, apparently. Travis's family-emergency leave has been extended. I'm not at liberty to share details. Shall we move on?"

"Fine." Lissa's mouth tightened into a thin line, the words forced from between clenched teeth.

"Tell me what prompted your call to Travis in the first place, so I can understand exactly what you expect from me." He scribbled her name and Bella's at the top of the paper. Glancing back at where Lissa had sat, he couldn't help but notice how easily he could read her expressions. He prepared himself to receive another diatribe of verbal dislike, realizing she hadn't changed much in that regard over the years.

Lissa took a deep breath. "As I explained to Travis, a dognapping ring has moved into the Charlotte area. There have been eleven dogs stolen in the last few weeks. All purebreds. Nobody knows what they're doing with the dogs, but one assumes they are being resold for breeding since there haven't been any ransom demands made. There is one thing I hadn't told Travis, mainly because I'm trying to convince myself I'm not crazy." She stood and walked across the room toward the fireplace.

"What's that?" Lissa wasn't acting all that confident at the moment.

She hesitated. "It's just that...sometimes, I feel like I'm being followed. I don't want to sound paranoid, but I can't seem to shake the feeling. Bella is like a baby to me, and I want her protected. I can't be with her twenty-four-seven."

Some would discount her feelings as paranoia, but Damien wasn't one of them. A good investigator paid attention to all details, even feelings, especially when he knew Lissa wasn't prone to an overly active imagination.

"I'm listening. Tell me what you have in mind?"

"When I need to put in time at the track for practice, or when I'm racing, or have marketing photo shoots or even meetings, I need you to keep her safe. That means she'll be with you when I'm unavailable. And that means you need to keep up with me so you're there when I need you. The live-in status is for the comfort of knowing someone is here to help me if I run into trouble. Three sets of ears to be proactive."

Maybe she has changed. The post-famous-parents Lissa wouldn't have held back from taking a shot at him. "Three?"

"Bella has ears, in case you haven't noticed. And she's quick to let me know if she doesn't like someone or if she hears something she doesn't recognize." The dog raised its head and looked between the two of them as her name continued to pop up.

"Well then, I guess it's a good thing she seems to like me." As if on cue, Bella jumped off the sofa and moseyed over to where Damien sat.

"Well, that makes one of us." Lissa's gaze followed Bella, her scowl deepening.

It would seem Lissa disliked competition on and off the racetrack. "So you expect me to follow you around like a puppy dog, pun intended, with the sole intention of babysitting Bella when you can't?" Bella jumped onto his lap and nuzzled his hand, looking for attention. Damien obliged, scratching behind her ears, a move he'd seen Lissa do a few times.

"You're a quick learner." Lissa smirked.

"Why can't Bella and I just stay here at the house, out of the limelight, and wait for you? It would make more sense."

"Because she typically goes with me everywhere. I'm not letting these dognappers change the way things are between her and I. She was abandoned before I rescued her at the shelter, and she has separation anxiety issues. I try to keep her as close as possible to avoid upsetting her."

Being face-to-face with the celebrity side of Lissa Walker was going to be a challenge, but one he swore he can handle. Travis had thought

Damien would be able to work from Lissa's house, knocking out his own caseload and covering for Travis, but his cousin had thought wrong.

"What's the agenda look like for today?" He resigned himself to the inevitable and had no choice but to do it her way. She was the client.

"Today, I have a practice day. I'm due at the track to meet with Mack, my crew chief, and my crew at eleven. We need to go over any issues with the changes they are making to my car before I practice. I've only got track time for an hour starting at noon and need to make the most of it."

Damien jotted down his notes. *11 to 1. Racetrack practice.* "What else?"

"That's it for today. Tomorrow, I've got a press conference at the Walton Hotel at noon followed by a luncheon."

"Your favorite thing." He hadn't meant to say that out loud.

"What's that supposed to mean?" She crossed her arms over her mid-section and glared at him.

"Just an observation. You do a lot of interviews." Damien jotted down the next entry on their to-do list.

"It comes with the territory. You wouldn't understand," she huffed.

"I understand far better than you think. It's just not a world I choose." End of subject. "Anything else?"

Lissa shot him an odd look, and if he hadn't been looking directly at her, he would've missed it. There was no telling what was going on in her head, but whatever it was, Damien was sure he wouldn't like it.

"Other than that, tomorrow's a light day. I'll be here at the house, and you can make yourself scarce. I'm sure you can find something to do." Her dismissive tone said it all.

Get lost so I don't even notice you're around. He was more than happy to accommodate her wishes with one minor exception. "One small problem. Tomorrow, I need off at ten-thirty. Can you hold up leaving until I get back around one?"

"What part of full-time don't you understand?" she snapped.

"The part where I'm filling in to help you out, and I already had plans. I'm asking you to work with me. Some things are very important to me, and everyone needs time off here and there. It's not an unreasonable expectation."

"I can just imagine." Lissa let out an exaggerated sigh.

"You of all people should understand."

"Fine. I'll get Bev to watch Bella until you're finished with your date. At least I can rely on her."

"Thanks. You know, you *can* rely on me too. I really am sorry if this puts a kink in your schedule. I'd change my plans if I could." It was easier to let her assume he was going on a date than to tell her the truth. Not many people knew he coached little league on the side, and he preferred to keep it that way. He didn't need Lissa to like him, just to work with him.

"Anything else I need to know about?" she asked.

"Not yet. I'm working on other arrangements for any other obligations I have."

"Thank you." It was the closest Lissa had come to being nice. He liked it.

"Now that we have that cleared up, are you good with keeping an eye on Bella for a bit? If you can tell me which room mine is, I can drop my stuff off and get settled. And then I need to go through the house and check out your security system." He stood, grabbed his bag, and slung it over his shoulder.

"She's fine with me. The only security is what you see at the front and back doors. I have cameras there, and the alarm sounds if the doors are opened at night after I've armed the system. I disarm them around six a.m. when I first wake up. The sound of the alarm going off all day with people coming and going can get irritating. As to your room, it's up the stairs, second on the right. There's a private bathroom."

"Sounds good. You won't have to worry about running into me wrapped in a towel and half naked after a shower." Damien chuckled. He couldn't help but goad her seeing as she was being nice and all.

"That would be a tragedy." Lissa's lips curled up at the sides as she seemed to lose the battle to fight against smiling. It softened her features, once again reminding him of the Lissa he once knew. Soft and sweet and incredibly attractive in a very unassuming way.

Damien went in search of his room. The rest of the house was meticulously designed in a contemporary style with a tan, black, and white theme throughout. The entire place could've been straight out of *House Beautiful* magazine. The room she'd given him was twice the size he would've expected, given that she didn't want him there. He'd half expected her to put him in a broom closet or the attic.

He spent the next hour making notes and jotting down information about what he needed to get the house up to speed with necessary security measures.

The extensive backyard and luxury pool added a lot of ground to cover, but by nightfall, he'd have everything in place.

Chapter Five

♥

DAMIEN FOUND LISSA IN the kitchen shortly before it was time to leave for the track. "I'm ready to go whenever you are. Should we take two cars?"

"You can ride with me. I promise I'm a safe driver." Lissa grinned.

He hoped she'd do more of it. Smiles looked good on her. "Your definition of safe and mine differ. If we ride together, how about I drive?"

"Sounds a little macho male to me." She made a face, daring him to deny the truth.

"It's nothing of the sort. It's called sanity."

"Try me. Then you can brag to all your friends that Lissa Walker personally chauffeured you to the racetrack. Think of all the publicity you'll get." There was an odd sarcastic note in her voice he hadn't heard before.

For some reason, he found himself wanting to agree. Not for bragging rights, but for the opportunity to see her in action firsthand. No matter how much he didn't want to like her, he couldn't help but admire her accomplishments.

"You're on, but with one condition. If I think you're crazy, you'll switch places and let me drive."

"Deal." It was the first thing they'd agreed on in forever. Hopefully, it wouldn't be the last.

Lissa picked up Bella and carried her out to the garage. Damien wasn't surprised to see a high-dollar performance sports car parked there, but it did make him pause and reconsider the deal. Especially when she slid behind the wheel of the Porsche and let Bella sit in her lap.

"Want me to hold her?" he offered.

"It would be great if you could, considering it's illegal and you're sitting in Bella's seat. She likes to look out the window."

She handed him the dog, who proceeded to doggy lick his face—something he could do without. He used the sleeve of his shirt to wipe his cheek.

Halfway to the track, Damien started to relax. Her need for speed clearly didn't trickle over into real life. Lissa drove the speed limit every inch of the way. "You don't seem like a speed demon. You drive like an old lady."

"It's called being safe. I like to be in control on the track and off. Out here it's more dangerous because you can never tell what the other drivers are doing or thinking. Going the speed limit gives me time to react."

"That makes sense." Damien nodded, forced to agree yet again. If they weren't careful, they might start agreeing on more and more things, and that would make it hard to keep up his dislike of her lifestyle.

It wasn't long before they arrived at the racetrack. After grabbing a duffel bag from the back seat and slinging it over her shoulder, Lissa grabbed Bella and put her in an oversized beach bag, the little dog's head hanging out over the edge.

"I've got to meet up with my crew. If you can take Bella, I'll have Andy, my manager, show you where to meet us if you decide you want to watch the practice. If not, you can just wander around and meet up with me back here at the car at two."

"You expect me to carry around a dog in a bag?" This just kept getting better.

"I do. It's the safest way for her to travel and for you to keep control over her. Bella's leash is at the bottom of the bag if you need to take her for a walk to go potty. She normally does a little whimper when it's time for her to do her business." She held out the bag and the dog, her gaze daring him to say no.

He wouldn't give her the satisfaction. Damien took the bag. "Looks like you're stuck with me for a while, Bella. Mommy's orders." The need to tease Lissa grew. He was finding it a more natural way to deal with his own discomfort.

"Very funny, wise guy." She shook her head and rolled her eyes at him.

"It's been a while since I've been here, I might just walk around and get a feel for the place. If

there's time, maybe we'll check out the action."
More than anything, he wanted to watch her
out on the track. The very knowledge that he
wanted to, was more than enough to make him
resist the urge.

They walked toward the building side by side.

"Since when did you stop following racing? It
was something you talked about nonstop back
in high school."

About the same time Lissa had started driving in the races, but he wasn't about to tell
her that little bit of information. "I just lost
interest." The truth was he was far too interested in watching her, and that irritated him
more than anything. He'd thought he'd moved
past his childhood crush, but his reaction to her
now proved otherwise, and he still had to get
through two weeks of living with her every day.

Lissa frowned. "Interesting. Before or after I
started racing?"

"Around the same time, I guess."

She stopped walking and pinned him with a
hard look, her brows scrunched up. "Coincidence or convenience?"

"You flatter yourself. Complete coincidence." It was the only answer he was willing to give. He pulled open the front door and let her pass inside before following.

Any answer she'd been about to say remained unsaid as a man approached them, waving and trying to get her attention.

"Lissa, darling, I'm glad you're here. We need to get down to the meeting. Stat. Mack and the others are waiting, and I don't want to waste any of your practice time. We need to fine tune how to handle turn four and see how the new tires are going to hold out."

"Hi, Andy. This is, Damien Trent, a friend of mine." He noticed her stumble over the introduction and that she hadn't advertised the reason for his presence.

The two men shook hands. "Nice to meet you."

"Damien's going to walk around and check out the track. Can you let him into the pit area if he shows up at the security point?"

"No problem. I'll leave him a pass with Harvey." Andy turned to Damien. "If you just tell our security guy your name, he'll take care of the rest. Lots of action even during practice."

"Thanks. I'll check it out." Damien readjusted

Bella. "Just depends what the little lady wants to do." Lissa scratched the dog behind her ears. "Mommy will be back. You be good for Damien."

Bella gave out a little yelp, her little doggy tongue licking Lissa's hand. The tinkling sound of Lissa's laugh was sweet music to his ears. It was a laugh he remembered from many years ago. The same laugh that had always made him want to kiss her. Unfortunately, it was having the same effect on him now.

"Oh, and one other thing. There are earplugs for Bella in the side pocket of the bag if you come down to the track, and you can get some from Harvey. Better to be safe, because it gets pretty loud down there."

Sweet and thoughtful. He was seeing a side of her he hadn't seen in a very long time.

Andy and Lissa headed down the hall to their meeting. Damien looked around, the sights and smells of the racetrack like a homecoming of sorts. He probably should have never given up his passion for racing but seeing Lissa as part of the package had soured his attraction to the sport. The few occasions he tried to watch, memories of the times they spent together, doing exactly the same thing, brought back the pain of losing her to the high school quarterback. Damien hadn't been good enough for the new social butterfly on the scene.

"Well, Bella, it's just the two of us. I'm sure we can find something to entertain us." He reached up and scratched behind Bella's ear. Judging by the way she cocked her head to one side, it was a favorite spot. Damien laughed and was rewarded with a doggy lick. He shook his head, finding it hard to believe he was toting around a dog at a racetrack. The guys at the office would have a field day if they saw this. Luckily, he'd sworn Travis to secrecy.

Damien walked around the track, stopping at various advantage points to watch the number twenty-three put his bright-yellow stock car to the paces on the track. Lissa's dark red stock car was on pit road, edging her way toward the track. She pulled out just after the yellow car entered the pit.

The roar of the engine reverberated through his body as she passed by, picking up speed as she hit the backstretch. He couldn't help but admire the way she handled the turns. If only she could have dealt with the turns in life as well as she did on the track, things might've been different for them.

"Bella, what do you say we head down to the pit area?" He adjusted the earplugs on the dog and made his way down to the security entrance.

He spotted Andy and waved. "I've decided to head down to the pit to watch if it's still okay?"

"Sure thing. Let me get you through security. You two close friends? I don't remember seeing you around before." Andy eyed him with interest.

"No. We knew each other in high school and then lost track. Ran into each other again recently, and I was interested in what she does." *More like yesterday.*

"You and most of racing America fans." He chuckled. "She doesn't trust very many people with Bella, so I reckon she trusts you quite a bit." Andy didn't have a clue.

"I guess so." It still felt silly toting a dog around in a bag over his shoulder, but Andy's comment made it a little less painful.

"Here you go. Harvey, this is the guy I left the pass for. Damien Trent."

"Sure thing." The man handed him the pass. "Enjoy."

"I've got to go back out, but if you follow this hall, you'll find where you need to go easily enough. Just ask otherwise."

"Thanks." Damien entered the pit area just as Lissa came racing around the track. The deafening roar of the engine sent adrenaline coursing through his body at speeds faster than her car. He had zero control over the situation. Lissa, on the other hand, was traveling at speeds over 200 mph, and she appeared in total control.

It was mind-boggling.

But her track record said she was good. Four wins and eight top-ten finishes to her career. She was one of the leading women drivers of all times, not to mention all the men she beat out to get there. He may have quit watching racing, but he'd never been able to stop himself from following her record.

Lap after lap, she raced around the track. Finally, she exited the track into the pit. She pulled herself up out of the car through the window and removed her helmet. She reached up and unwound the hair tie, her long hair falling into place as she shook the brown locks down around her shoulders. The smile on her face was an honest reflection of the joy she got from racing.

Several other cars were in the pit area, their drivers all standing together in a group off to the side talking. Lissa glanced over at the men and then turned away. She spoke with her crew, her hands gesturing toward the car, more than likely discussing performance issues. Lissa was a true professional, and his admiration rose another notch seeing her in action from this close.

Lissa walked toward the watercooler area and grabbed a cup. She was joined by one of the guys from the group.

Damien couldn't help but notice her smile disappeared. Her body language had gone defensive. He took a few steps in her direction, trying to assess the situation. Raised voices reached his ears. Bella growled.

"My sentiments exactly, girl. Think we should join the conversation?" He patted Bella's head and moved closer, but neither Lissa nor the other man seemed to notice his approach. The discussion grew louder, more heated. Every muscle in Damien's body went on alert.

"I told you to leave me alone, Razor. If you've got issues, they're your own."

"My issue is you. You don't belong out here taking up a spot and causing crashes that wipe out the chances of real drivers." The man snarled at Lissa; his posture more threatening than Damien cared for.

"I raced the same qualifiers as you, and the board doesn't have a problem with women drivers. If you have a problem with me driving, I suggest you talk to them. And as to crashing, you should look to your own weaknesses. Maybe you're the one who doesn't belong out there." Lissa wasn't backing down.

The man moved closer. "You little—"

"Mister, you might want to check your attitude." Damien jumped in, unwilling to stand by and let this jerk threaten Lissa.

At the sound of his voice, Lissa swung around, her angry gaze meeting his head on. "Stay out of this, Damien."

"I see how it is. Not so tough are you, Maneater?" Razor snarled. He turned to face Damien. "You might want to do as the little...*umm*...lady says and stay out of something that doesn't concern you." The way he said *lady* wasn't a compliment.

"Anything that concerns Miss Walker concerns me." He wasn't backing down, even if there'd be heck to pay later with Lissa.

"Damien, I can handle this on my own. I don't need your interference." The steel of her voice lashed against his skin. Her finger poked him in the chest. "You forget, you were hired to be my doggy guard. *Not my* bodyguard. So, stick to protecting Bella and leave me alone. You're only making things worse."

"A doggy guard?" Razor walked away laughing at him.

Lissa's reminder had made him look like a fool, putting him in his place. That's what he got for trying to help the Maneater.

"Here." He held out Bella so Lissa could take her precious baby. "You're done practicing and it appears you're free to take care of her again."

"Fine. I'll meet you at the car when I'm ready." Lissa walked away, leaving him standing there. She was always the first to leave, and nothing had changed.

Left with no choice, he followed her down the hall. *Like a puppy dog.* The thought did little to put him in a better mood, much the same as the photographers taking pictures. He was nothing more than a lackey for the rich and famous Lissa Walker. This wasn't what he had signed on for. His privacy was his own, and he did his best to stay out of the limelight, considering he was in the security business.

Bev joined them as they exited the building. The two women walked close together; their heads tilted toward one another as they talked. Lissa stopped and turned back to face him.

"I prefer to talk to Bev alone." She tossed him her set of keys. "Think you can handle getting my car home in one piece and without a scratch?"

"Minutes ago, you said I was your doggy guard. I'm not sure valet is listed as one of my job duties per our contract, and I wouldn't want to overstep my bounds." Lissa was as spoiled as they came, and he wasn't about to let her get away with it.

"I would have thought you'd jump at the chance to drive the Porsche. Nothing like the old Jeep you drive around in."

"It's almost a classic, and I happen to love it. I don't need fancy or expensive to make a statement."

Lissa scowled. "Just because I can afford nice things doesn't make me a snob. You know nothing about me, so don't presume to judge."

"I know enough, and it's more than I want to know."

"Maybe you can't drive a stick? Or handle a sports car? Maybe you're not up to the challenge."

"Trying to bait me isn't going to work. Maybe it does on other people, but I'm not like the groupies that follow you around ready to do your bidding."

"Hey, you two. This is getting old, and I have somewhere to be."

Bev pulled Damien to the side. "The truth is, she's mad as a hornet at you and needs a little space. So, either take the Porsche or take my car, but give her some time to cool off."

"Women," he scoffed. "She should be mad at the guy she called Razor, not me. I was just trying to help. See if I do that again." The truth was he wanted to drive the car. He wasn't the kind of guy who would ever own one, but it didn't mean he was immune to the thrill of handling all the power under the hood.

Damien tossed the keys in the air and smiled. It was time for a little fun.

Thirty minutes later he pulled into the driveway, only to discover Lissa and Bev on the steps, Bella close by. The worried expression on Lissa's face spoke volumes. *It was just a car, for Pete's sake.*

"About time you got here." Lissa held out her hand for the keys.

Bev had worked her magic, and Lissa was no longer spitting fire, but she was far from relaxed. "I got lost."

"That doesn't surprise me. Simple tasks appear to be an issue for you." He shrugged.

Lissa turned, headed up the stairs, and back inside, leaving him and Bev staring after her.

Bev put her arm on his to stop him from following. "Try not to antagonize her. Between the dognapper, the endorsements, the charity, the upcoming race, and, yes, a few chauvinistic males, she's really stressed. But she's dealing with it all the best she can. Her way. I've promised her fewer appointments after the race, but for now, we must follow through with the commitments we have scheduled."

"Why would she want less of them? She loves the attention." Maybe Lissa's friend could enlighten him about some things that didn't add up about her.

"Shows how much you know." Bev shook her head and rushed after Lissa.

He picked Bella up and cradled her in his arms.

"You know I'm right about her, don't you, girl?" Damien scratched Bella's head behind her ears, receiving a dog tongue bath in return. He smiled at her, loving her sweet disposition, but wondering how she'd gotten it with Lissa as an owner.

Damien walked into the living room, and the two women quit talking.

"I've got to run," Bev said. "Make sure you two don't kill each other." She glanced between them as if to confirm she was doing the right thing in leaving.

"We'll be fine." Lissa smiled. The transition was remarkable.

After Bev left, Damien waited for the return of the Maneater and was surprised when she didn't immediately appear.

"We don't have anything else for the night planned, so you're free to do what you want here. There's a media room upstairs with every movie you could imagine, and of course, video games. There's a gym next to it, and a pool out back if you're interested. There's also a library, but you don't look like the reading type." Whatever Bev had said to her had worked wonders.

"Thanks. And I do read, for your information." But she already knew that about him. Unless she'd honestly forgotten the times when they'd closeted themselves in a room just to read, shutting out the world and the stress that came with it.

"Who's your favorite author? Stephen King?"

Most guys liked King's novels, but they were a bit heavy for his tastes. "Hardly. Sir Arthur Conan Doyle, for starters."

"Really?" Her brows pulled together, the lines deepening across her forehead. "I like his writing, too."

"I remember. You used to read Sherlock Holmes *all* the time."

"You remember?" Her gaze intensified, and her head cocked to one side.

"I remember a lot of things. Whether I like it or not." He shouldn't have added the last part. She was being nice, and he'd been a jerk.

"Same here." She turned to walk away and then paused to turn back. Lissa took a deep breath.

"Look, I'm sorry about snapping at you earlier. That guy Razor is a pain in the behind. I get tired of dealing with it, but racing is a man's world, and I've learned to live in it. I know you were just trying to help, but guys like that will spin tales to the others, and it will only make it worse, not better."

She looked honestly contrite, and Damien's heart melted a little. He took a step toward her. "I'm sorry I interfered. But you shouldn't have to put it up with it, and it bothered me." Damien would have stepped in to help any woman, but especially Lissa. The idea of anyone upsetting her tore at his heart.

"Careful, or I might think you care."

It might be too late for that. "I'll be careful, don't worry. Wouldn't want to give you any false impressions."

Lissa grinned. "Duly noted. Since we have that settled, and we've agreed there's no love lost between us, what would you say to eating dinner with me? I can order something as my way of an apology, and we can be non-friends hanging out to pass the evening."

Lissa was showing him the down-to-earth side of her personality, something he recognized from back in high school. If she was trying to impress him, it was working. Too bad he liked what he saw. Especially the little heart-shaped birthmark on the side of her neck he saw as she pushed her hair back over her shoulder. He'd once told her it was her destiny stamp of love.

"I wouldn't pass up the bribe. But no hoity-toity food."

"Hoity-toity? Did you really just say that?" She laughed. "How about pizza and wine?"

"How about beer?"

"How about wine? At least it's red. I don't drink beer, so there's none in the house."

"A race car driver who doesn't drink beer? I'm shocked." He smiled, laying his hand over his chest to emphasize his words.

"You might be shocked at a lot of things, but I promise not to bore you with the details." She laughed.

"Well, then I accept. I'd like to go get in a quick workout and then a shower. Want to meet back downstairs in about an hour?"

"Make it an hour and a half, and I'll join you. I've got some bookwork to take care of and I'll keep Bella with me."

"Fine. It's a date. *A non-friend date,*" he corrected.

Chapter Six

♥

IT WAS THE SAME Lissa staring back at her in the mirror, but she felt different. Damien always seemed to keep her emotions on a roller coaster proving nothing had changed since high school.

After stripping down, she stepped under the hot spray, eager to rinse off the sticky sweat clinging to her skin from an afternoon spent on the track.

The water was warm and pleasant, easing the tension in her shoulders and neck. It had been a spontaneous offer to suggest they share dinner, but the last thing she'd expected was for Damien to agree. Friend or not, she was looking forward to the evening with him. Probably far more than she should.

Lissa came out of the bathroom to see Bella sound asleep on the bed, sprawled out like she didn't have a care in her doggy world. *Too bad, it wasn't true.* Lissa would be relieved when the dognappers were caught and behind bars.

After careful consideration, she chose her favorite blue jeans, the pair with a few holes and a patch on the knee. Well-worn but comfortable—and comfort was definitely in order tonight. She chose a Caribbean-blue-green shirt to wear, a color she'd been told complimented the blue of her eyes. The three-quarter length sleeve cotton shirt fit around her chest but hung loosely from the bodice line, the material softly caressing against her bare skin.

For some reason, it was necessary for her to show Damien the real Lissa Walker, something she didn't do with just anyone. It would do no good to analyze why, but if she had to guess, it would be because deep down, she still cared. Why else would she let her guard down?

She slipped on a pair of flats to match her shirt and then set about styling her hair, taking extra care to make her long, wavy curls frame her face. There was no sense in not looking her best while she entertained Damien. The feminine side of her was unable to resist the lure. He looked great after all these years. The mature Damien was an even greater heartthrob than the schoolboy she'd once known.

Lissa finished getting ready and called in the pizza order before heading downstairs. She grabbed a bottle of wine, removed the foil wrapping that covered the top, and twisted the corkscrew down into the cork before giving it a hard tug to remove it.

It didn't budge. She tried again, but the corkscrew slipped back out. *Not now.*

Bella barked at Damien as he came down the stairs.

Lissa tried a third time, making the hole slightly to the side. She strained as she pulled, but the stupid cork wouldn't give an inch.

Damien walked into the kitchen.

"Need help?"

"As much as I hate to admit it, yes. It's one of those newfangled plastic corks I hate. Sometimes they get wedged in so hard a normal person can't remove it." She handed him the bottle, tired of dealing with it. So much for her ego.

"I'm surprised you don't have one of those automatic openers. This—" he held up her opener, "— surprises me. It's archaic."

"But normally the most reliable." Lissa moved to get two glasses out of the cupboard.

"Let's hope you're right." Damien pulled the cork out on the first try. "Weakling." He grinned.

"Thanks. Your attempt to be funny is what's weak. We both know I'm in good shape. I have to be to do six hundred laps on a racetrack and win. Clearly, I loosened it for you." It was her turn to smile.

"Good point."

She poured the wine, and they sat at the counter, one barstool separating them as they turned to each other to talk.

Lissa took a sip of wine. It needed to breathe about fifteen minutes before the flavors would explode into their full potential, but waiting wasn't an option. She could handle her car on the racetrack, Damien was another story. He made her nervous.

An awkward silence fell between them.

Damien took a sip of wine. "Not bad. Did you order the pizza yet?"

"I did. It should be here in about twenty minutes."

"Good. I'm hungry."

"Me, too." The small talk was killing her.

"This is a little awkward. We need an icebreaker, or this is going to be a long night."

"I agree. Why don't you start by telling me what you've been doing since high school? How did you end up in the security business?" There was a lot she wanted to know, but his job was the safest topic. At least for now.

Damien's expression grew cold, his scowl a good indicator the topic wasn't as safe as she'd hoped.

"I ended up doing security because computer hackers stole information from my father's company while I was in college, and he was framed to take the rap. I know my father. He can be over- bearing at times, but he's not a thief. I didn't think the police were doing a good job, and I started researching some things on my own, with the help of some guys at the university. One thing led to another, and we broke up the hacking ring. My father was released from prison, but by then, the blow to his career and life was major. He had to basically start over."

"Oh my gosh. I'm so sorry. After I left town for college, I never came back until after I graduated, and I've never heard anything about it. How's your dad now?"

Lissa knew the media would have had a field day. They always did. She'd learned early on to play it their way if she wanted to stay on their good side. One slip. One rumor. Careers washed up overnight. They could be ruthless if you didn't play by the rules.

"He's fine. They cut back, moved into a smaller place, and I think they're happier. Dad's not a workaholic anymore and is spending more time with Mom and the family. The publicity was pretty bad and not something I'd ever want to relive."

"It can be. But you learn to live with it. There's a lot of good that comes with the territory as well as the bad."

"It's not a lifestyle I would choose."

Lissa got the point. She and Damien would have never worked out even if they had dated, so things had turned out exactly the way they needed to. They were as mismatched a pair as orange and red socks. "What kind of cases do you take besides dog sitting?" Lissa felt the need to tease him, hoping to lighten the mood.

"Very funny. Mostly computer technology issues. Information hacking, dark web, corporate espionage, that sort of thing." He took a sip of wine and settled back against the chair.

"Sounds exciting. Not. Computers and I don't like each other much." She laughed. Actually, she and computers had more of a love-hate relationship. "Travis seems to like what he's doing. We've talked a few times over the years, mostly when I run into him somewhere, which is what made me think of him for the job. I hope his mother is okay." Lissa made a mental note to call

Travis later. She should have already called him to check up on his mother.

"She pulled through the surgery fine and is in recovery. Travis will be back here to help you out before you know it. Don't worry." Damien let out a deep sigh, leaving her to wonder what he was thinking.

"I'm not worried. For two non-friends, we're doing good having dinner together. I reckon we can muddle our way through the rest of our time together." Surprisingly, she was enjoying herself, and it left her hoping he felt the same. But getting any kind of feedback from him was like trying to harness the RPMs of an engine. *Impossible.*

"Good. It's not like we have a choice. What's your story? I remember you went off to college, but I thought I heard you went for business and planned on joining your family's empire. Racing isn't even remotely close." There it was again. Barely detectable, but his voice had a slightly disparaging note to it.

"I did go to study business. My parents wanted me to manage the financial aspects of the company, and I ended up getting my MBA at Kent State in Ohio. But after coming home, I realized it wasn't what I wanted to do. By then, I'd been dabbling in racing as a hobby, and I decided to pursue it as a career. I've done well and don't regret my decision." It wouldn't always be this way, but for now, it gave her the freedom to live her own life, and the money and connections came in handy for the things she found important. Like the rescue shelter.

"Kent State? Impressive. But then so is your track record." A glimmer of admiration showed on his face.

More shocking was the knowledge that Damien had followed her career on the track.

The doorbell rang; the pizza man's arrival poor timing as far as Lissa was concerned. She wanted to know more, her curiosity in overdrive. "Hold that thought while I get our pizza." She stood and crossed to the table to grab her purse.

"I've got this one." Damien was already headed down the hallway.

Another nice gesture.

It wasn't long before he returned, pizza in hand, and Bella happily following him. *Traitor.* But who could blame her?

Damien and Lissa were two very different people, but apparently, those differences had nothing to do with the attraction she was still feeling seven years later.

"Smells good. Put it here on the table, and we can take our plates to the living room."

"Works for me."

They each took two slices, a napkin, and grabbed their wine, Damien following her into the living room.

"Should we watch a movie?" Lissa asked, sitting down and grabbing the remote.

Much to her surprise, Damien sat down next to her. "Sure. If you pick a murder mystery, I'll be on board."

"You're too easy."

"Not if you had said a documentary," he teased, leaning forward, but then stopping short. "Sorry. I've never been on an un- friend date, and I'm not exactly sure of the rules."

"That makes two of us." She grinned.

Lissa had been sure he was going to kiss her, and she'd been sure she wanted him to. But where would that leave them tomorrow?

Chapter Seven

♥

LISSA POURED A CUP of coffee and sat down at the kitchen table. Her feet were cold against the tiled floor, but she'd always looked at it as invigorating. Part of waking up. It was the same way with her pajamas, except for this morning. As adverse as she was to wear a robe, she'd do it. Giving up her habit of running around her jammies all morning wasn't a treat she'd give up. Not even for Damien.

She looked like a fluffy snow bunny, but it would have to do. At least she couldn't be accused of trying to be flirty. Lissa laughed, wondering exactly what he would do if she'd come down in her normal granny-plaid pajamas. She'd never know, which was probably a good thing. At least he'd signed the confidentiality agreement, and she didn't have to worry about pictures splashed across the front pages. For as public as her life may seem, her private life was her own, and something she valued highly.

Today she didn't have to be at the conference and luncheon until noon, which meant hair and makeup could wait. Until the last second, if possible. She may have run a brush through her hair, but that was the extent of preening for her houseguest.

Bella ran around the room playing with her toy, full of morning energy and trying to motivate Lissa to join in her fun. "Not yet, girl. Let me wake up." Lissa laughed, picking up the toy Bella dropped at her feet, and tossed it across the room.

Damien strolled into the kitchen and helped himself to the coffee. "Good morning." Men had it easy. Roll out of bed, toss on a pair of jeans and a T-shirt, and bam, they looked good. His seven-a.m. scruff only served to enhance his macho appeal.

"Morning. I trust you slept well." Lissa smiled.

Last night had erased the tension between them, and somehow, they'd come to a middle-ground place of truce.

Bella came running to greet him and dropped the toy to see if she could find a new play partner.

"I did. Thanks for asking." He picked up the toy and gave it a toss.

Bella had a new friend, and for some reason, Lissa didn't mind as much as she had at first. Her dog was a good judge of character, and therefore, she was more than willing to give Damien the benefit of the doubt. "Nice robe." He grinned.

"What's wrong with it? It's comfortable."

"It looks hot, that's what," he said, his tone totally serious.

"Ha-ha. Would you prefer I walked around in my granny plaid nightgown?" She should have kept her mouth shut.

"Umm, what kind of question is that? Either one sounds hot."

Lissa blushed at his response. It was like high school all over again. Before he'd broken his promise about taking her to the prom. And before he'd asked her best friend to go instead. This was flirting, an art she'd never really perfected.

"Oh, wait a minute. You thought...yikes." He grinned. "I meant...it looks like it would be warm. You keep the room hot. The room temperature." Damien shook his head and laughed. "Sorry, this is coming out all wrong. Maybe a change in subject? Forget I said anything." Of course, he wanted a change in subject. He'd lost interest in her when they were in high school, and apparently, some things didn't change. Although for a moment, he'd managed to let her remember.

"Last night was unexpectedly fun. I still can't believe you like murder mysteries." She took a sip of coffee, trying to hide her unsettled emotions.

"Why? I'm in security." Damien sat down next to her and picked up the newspaper.

"Computer security. That's a far cry from murder." She laughed.

"It's all about solving a crime." He smiled; one eyebrow raised as if he was confused how she could miss the connection. "Don't forget I need to leave at ten-thirty."

And just like that, the camaraderie between them dissipated, his words a sharp reminder of something she'd chosen not to remember. "I had forgotten. Are you sure you can't change your plans? Bev's not going to be happy with her extra duties, and I simply can't take the chance and leave Bella at home alone."

"Sorry. I honestly would if I could, but it's not that simple."

Of course, it's not. Wouldn't want to cancel his date.

"Pleasure before business. I get it. If you don't focus on your job, you'll never get ahead. Is that why you got stuck covering Travis's contract? Low man on the SDS totem pole?"

Damien shot her a weird look. "Probably." He picked up his cup and headed for the door. "I've got a few things to take care of before I go. I'll be back here no later than one o'clock to relieve Bev."

"Fine. Not much choice in the matter it would seem." Lissa watched as Bella followed him out of the kitchen, the door swinging into place just as after she cleared the opening.

Traitor.

Lissa fixed herself a quick breakfast of poached eggs and toast, with a glass of orange juice. More than enough to hold her over until the luncheon. The meeting was to go over the last-minute details for the charity event and the expectations of her role in making it a success. The animal rescue shelter was a cause Lissa wholeheartedly believed in, and it was the one area of her life she didn't mind the demands it placed on her time.

Bella was a rescue corgi. Abandoned in a barn, she'd been left to make her own way in the world when the owners had moved away. Only two years old, she'd been hungry and afraid. If Lissa could, she'd take in more pets than just Bella, but for now, one was all she could handle in light of her schedule. One day, when she quit racing, she'd surround herself with rescue animals. Their love and devotion were far more appealing and trustworthy than the two-legged variety of animals.

"Bella!" It wasn't that she minded her dog hanging out with Damien, but Lissa needed to get some work done. It would be easier to concentrate knowing Bella was curled up in a corner in her office than to have to deal with Damien again before he left.

She went up the stairs and called again. "Bella!"

Playful barks echoed down the hall as her baby raced toward her. Lissa leaned down to pick her up as Damien stepped into the hallway.

"I'm just checking to see where she went. I'll be leaving soon and wanted to make sure you knew you were on point to watch Bella."

"That's fine. Enjoy your date."

"Sure thing." He started to turn away and go back into the room, but then stopped and looked back at her. "Lissa, it's not what you think."

"It doesn't matter what I think. And you certainly don't have to explain yourself. I just hope we don't have too many more of these interruptions." Her crisp tone sounded petty. The problem was, she didn't want to hear about his exploits with women.

But it was the reason she didn't want to know that upset her the most.

His expression hardened, but he didn't say a word. He simply walked away, closing the door behind him. Hard.

Lissa spent the next hour going over her books, most of it with Bella curled up in her lap fast asleep. She heard Damien's bedroom door close and the sound of his footsteps retreating down the hall. He was leaving. It was a sudden reminder she'd gotten caught up in bookwork and had failed to call Bev to come and babysit Bella.

Lissa picked up her phone and hit the speed dial for Bev, relieved when her friend picked up after the first ring. "I'm glad you answered. I'm in a bit of a fix this afternoon, and I know I can't cancel my afternoon appointments."

"What's wrong? Is it Bella or the hunky doggy guard watching over her?"

"Ha-ha. It's both. I wouldn't have a problem if that so-called hunky doggy guard would actually do his job." Lissa let out a sigh that would have set a pinwheel to spinning.

"Now what's the problem?"

"He's off on another date, of course. I need you to watch Bella for me. You know I can't take her to the restaurant. The owners would have a hissy fit. Not to mention, she's not the best with people shoving mics in my face or up-close flash photography."

"Aren't you supposed to be there at noon? I can't do it. I have a meeting across town with a new client. It's taken me a month to get the appointment. I'm sorry, but I can't cancel now."

This was a disaster. Bev would help if she could, and it really wasn't her fault. The problem lay at the feet of her newly hired doggy guard. "I should have known this wouldn't work."

"I'm sorry. You know I would watch her if I could."

"I know. I'll think of something. Good luck with your client. I hope you get the account."

Lissa hung up the phone and tried to figure out what else she could do. She glanced over at Bella, who was still fast asleep. There was no way she was leaving her alone. Which meant she'd have to cancel. Everyone would be furious, but Bella was more important.

She looked up the number of the restaurant and started to dial. The phone rang several times as Lissa's gaze scanned her calendar. Bella's grooming appointment was next week, the date circled in red as a reminder. The phone was answered by the restaurant's machine. Lissa waited for the recording to finish to leave a message.

Groomer.

Lissa hit the end button, terminating the call. She dialed the grooming clinic. Trying to change her appointment time was worth a shot.

"Radcliffe's Grooming, the place where your pets are treated like family. How may I help you?" The warm, friendly greeting gave Lissa hope this would work out.

"This is Lissa Walker. Is Angie in?"

"Hello, Ms. Walker. She sure is. Hold one second, and I'll get her."

"Thank you." Just getting her groomer on the phone was half the battle.

"Lissa, this is Angie. How are you?" Bella's personal groomer for the past four years came on the phone.

"I've got a problem, and I'm hoping you can help me."

"Always. You and Bella are some of my favorite clients."

"Thank you. I know our appointment is set for next week but is there any way you can come today? Like soon. I'm sorry it's so last minute, but the person I was going to have stay with Bella isn't available. I thought if I could get her grooming done, it would take care of two things at once."

"What time? I'll check the computer."

"I have to be somewhere at noon, so if you could be here at let's say 11:30, that would be great."

"Wow. Today must be your lucky day. I had a cancellation. It'll be more like 11:45 when we get there because I've got one other appointment ahead of you. I'll be bringing my new assistant, Teresa. Will that give you enough time?"

"Barely. But I'll make it work. You're a lifesaver. Give Bella the works. I'm sure she'll love it. Oh, and Damien Trent will be here this afternoon at one to take over watching her." Lissa breathed a sigh of relief. This was going to work out after all.

"Perfect. See you both soon. Don't you worry, I'll take good care of Bella." Angie hung up, and Lissa shot off a text to Damien to let him know the change of plans.

Lissa: Bev can't make it. Angie from Radcliff's Grooming Clinic is coming instead. She'll be here at 11:45 and will be expecting you by one p.m.

Damien: Gotcha

Not a real talkative guy, but what did she expect?

It took her the better part of an hour to pick out her outfit and do her hair and makeup. She'd learned long ago not to leave the house looking anything less than perfect. Pictures had a way of surfacing everywhere, the good, the bad, and the ugly. Sometimes she wondered if the gossip papers paid bonus money for the bad ones. But it was all for a good cause, and that's what was most important.

Lissa finished getting ready and was watching the video of her last practice track run when the doorbell rang. Bella jumped down from the couch and ran toward the door barking.

She pulled open the door but was surprised to find someone other than Angie standing there. "May I help you?"

The woman smiled. "Yes, I'm Teresa Sanders. Angie's new assistant." The woman handed her a card. "She was running late with her last appointment and asked me to come here and get started until she can arrive. She didn't want you to be late for your luncheon."

Lissa inspected the business card, satisfied Teresa was with Radcliffe's Grooming Clinic. Besides, how else would she have known about the luncheon and Angie's change of plans?

"That's great. I'm glad you could make it. I really do need to get going."

She fished out her own business card from her purse and handed it to Teresa. "Call my cell phone if you need me for anything. And tell Angie I said thanks. I'll settle with her later."

"Don't worry about a thing. I'll start Bella's bath, and she'll be fine. Dogs love pamper grooming."

"So true." She smiled at her baby, who sat at her feet eyeing the newcomer. Bella was acting strange, parked at her feet and not making a move to check out the newcomer. Once Angie got here, she'd be better. Lissa picked Bella up, gave her a quick hug and kiss and set her back down. "Be good for Teresa and Angie, and I'll be home before you know it." She patted Bella on the head and then made her way to the garage, anxious to get to the restaurant on time. She expected people to respect her time, and she believed in treating others the same way.

Damien pulled into the driveway and up to the front of the house. He glanced at his watch, relieved to see it was only 12:55. Five minutes to spare, giving Lissa zero reason to call him out for his inadequacies again.

He slid out of the jeep and headed for the porch, keys in hand if needed. He tried the handle, found the door unlocked and pushed it open, stepping inside.

"Hello. Anybody here?" He didn't want to scare the groomer and figured a courtesy holler was in order.

Damien walked down the hall into the living room and glanced around. No sign of the groomer or the dog. He'd gotten used to Bella coming running whenever she heard his voice. It was kind of cute.

"Bella!" He tried again before heading for the kitchen to check there. Still nothing. Bella was probably in a bathtub enjoying the extra attention. He headed up the stairs to check on his charge. He entered all the rooms except Lissa's bedroom but found no sign of the dog or the groomer.

A stirring of unease settled in the pit of his stomach. He knocked on Lissa's door, unwilling to barge if she'd come home early and was napping with Bella.

When she didn't answer, he opened the door slowly, not wanting any surprises. He glanced around the room, noting the soft, feminine furnishings. Shades of purple and green graced the room, from the curtains to the bedspread, even the vase of flowers on the dresser. It was the only room that didn't match the rest of the showpiece. It was like seeing a very personal side of Lissa—a side of her that didn't match her Maneater image at all.

Now wasn't the time to think about what he was seeing, because what he didn't see far outweighed everything else. There was no sign of Lissa or Bella.

"Bella? Lissa?" he called out, just to be sure.

Damien took the steps two at a time and headed downstairs, anxious to check outside. Nothing. Adrenaline raced through his body as the knot of fear in his stomach grew by leaps and bounds with each step he took. He headed for the garage. Nothing.

Something isn't right. He hoped it was a simple matter of Lissa having had a change of plans and forgetting to tell him. He'd wring her neck for worrying him, but the alternative was not something he wanted to consider.

He pulled out his phone and swiftly typed out a text.

Damien: Has there been a change of plans you forgot to mention?

He didn't have to wait long for the answer.

Lissa: No. Why? Is something wrong?"

Damien: Maybe

His phone lit up, Lissa's name splashed across the screen, the loud ring harsh in the echo of the hallway.

"What do you mean maybe?" Lissa asked, fear evident with every word she spoke.

"There is no sign of your groomer or Bella. I've looked everywhere." Damien didn't want to alarm her any more than necessary, but the facts didn't look right.

"There must be some mistake. Check again. Angie should be there. I'm leaving now, and I'll call her while you check." The angst in her voice made him wince.

"Roger that." He hung up and started to recheck the entire house. In every closet, behind every door. Minutes later, his phone rang again.

"Damien, please tell me you found her?" The fear in Lissa's voice put a stranglehold on him because he knew his answer wasn't what she wanted to hear. "I'm sorry, Lissa. There is no one here. What did you find out?"

"No. No. No. It's not possible." The anguish in her voice gutted him.

"Lissa. Tell me." It's not that he didn't already know what she was going to say, but he needed to hear the words.

"Angie said she got a message that I had a change of plans and not to come. And Teresa, her assistant, is with her. The woman I left Bella with was a fake." Lissa sobbed into the phone.

"Are you driving right now?" He didn't want her behind the wheel of a car in the emotional state she was in. He needed to pick her up.

"Yes," she said through her sniffles.

There was nothing he could do but stay put at this point and wait. "Stay focused on your driving. I'll see you in a few minutes, and we can figure out what to do together. Don't worry, Lissa, we'll get her back. I promise." It was a promise he wasn't sure he could keep, but it was one she needed to hear.

"I can't believe I was such an idiot. Bella trusted me. And I let her down. I should have just canceled the luncheon. Nothing is as important as Bella."

It was hard for Damien to hear her like this. Lissa was a woman always in control, but right now, she was anything but.

If he'd done his job, this wouldn't have happened. And knowing Lissa the way he did, he didn't think it would take long for her to figure that out and transfer the blame.

When that happened, there'd be fireworks—and not the pretty Fourth of July kind.

Chapter Eight

♥

LISSA RACED HOME, SKIDDING to a stop at the front of her house. She didn't want to waste time parking in the garage and sitting still wasn't an option. There had to be some clue what happened to Bella.

Her poor baby.

It was killing her to think of how these people would treat Bella, and the fear she might not ever see her again continued to grow. She pushed the negative thoughts side, knowing it wouldn't get her anywhere.

Whoever had taken Bella was in for a rude awakening, because Lissa would never stop searching until she found her.

She ran into the house, letting the door slam shut behind her. The clip-clop of her heels echoed down the hall as loudly as her heart pounded in her ears. "Damien," she hollered.

From the minute she'd hung up the phone with Angie, her anger toward him had grown by leaps and bounds.

"You're home. I'm so sorry." He stepped toward her; arms outstretched.

And for the space of a second, she wanted nothing more than wrap herself in those strong arms and give in to the emotional rollercoaster consuming her. To let someone else be in control for just a moment.

Lissa snapped out of fantasy land and pulled up short, hands on her hips. "You're darn right you're sorry. If you'd been doing your job, Bella would be home safe and sound. This is all your fault!" She poked her finger into his chest, emphasizing the point. "I knew better than to trust you. You couldn't be counted on in high school, and you can't be counted on now. I should've never listened to Bev." She fought back the wave of tears threatening to spill over. Not now, not in front of Damien.

"The blame game isn't going to find Bella, and we need to work together to make it happen.

She sank down on the couch and let the tears that she'd been holding back fall. Lissa spotted a stuffed toy on the floor. Scooping it up, she clutched it to her chest. Bella's favorite toy—her gingerbread man.

Damien came to stand next to her, placing his hand on her shoulder. "I'm sorry."

A fresh wave of tears poured down her face.

"We need to call the police and file a report." His words were like ice on her emotions.

"No. No police. There have been a dozen dogs stolen in the last two weeks, and not one has been recovered. To my knowledge, they have zero leads. I'm not convinced they're doing any-thing to stop these guys, and I'm beginning to wonder if someone's working on the inside to keep it that way." She'd kept these thoughts to herself, but now the dognapping case had become more personal.

"Sounds to me like you don't trust them. Any reason in particular?"

Smart guy. Got it in one guess. "Nothing other than my belief they're incompetent. I thought about this on the way over, and I want to search for her on my own, or with your help if you agree. I've got money, and I'm willing to spread some around to buy information. I figure you know best where to look and who to talk to. Besides, I figure you owe me." She crossed her arms over her chest, hoping he would agree. If not, she'd don a costume and go it alone. But one way or the other, she was going after Bella.

"I don't know if not bringing them in on this is such a wise choice."

"But if I put this out there publicly, every criminal out there will jump on the bandwagon and start throwing me false hope for Bella's return at a price."

"You have a point there. No matter what happens between you and me, I intend to help find Bella. I know you think I'm incompetent and wasn't doing my job, but I put several security systems in place. Surveillance cameras will give us a picture of the woman who showed up, which is a good lead. And with a little luck, you won't have to spend a fortune or a lot of time to find her." Damien smiled.

Who smiled at a time like this? "What's that supposed to mean?" Lissa met his unwavering gaze.

"I installed a chip on her collar just this morning. We need to get the program set up on the computer, and then we should be able to get a pretty good idea of where she's at."

It took a few seconds for his words to register. "You're kidding? Oh my gosh, that's amazing." She jumped up and hugged Damien, his arms coming around her. "I can't believe you'll be able to track her. I love you. I love you. I love you." She kissed him on the mouth before pulling away and twirling about, sheer joy dancing through her veins.

The look of confusion on his face was enough to slow the dance a bit. "I'm sorry. Don't worry. I didn't mean that the way it sounded. I love you for being smart enough to put the collar on her. Okay, that's not right, either. I meant...I meant..."

"Don't worry. I think I understand. You're just happy. Really happy."

"Exactly." For years, she'd wondered how it would have felt if they'd taken their friendship to the natural next level—to be in his arms. She'd expected nice, but what she got was safety, warmth, and a feeling of coming home.

Right now, wasn't the time to dwell on it though, but later, when this was over, it would definitely be something to consider. "I take back everything I said. The mean things." She grinned. "So, what do we do first?"

He nodded as if coming to a decision, but he also didn't bother to explain.

"I need you to understand the system has its limitations, but I'm hoping we can make this work. I need to get the program loaded and running, and I'll need to get SDS to give me secure access to it. It doesn't always pinpoint to an exact location, but it can narrow it down quite a bit. If Bella has that collar on, we've got a great shot at finding her."

"That's awesome. Let's do this."

"You realize though if we locate Bella, we need to call in the police. These guys aren't going to take too kindly to us barging in, taking Bella, and exposing their location. These are criminals, and this will be dangerous. I don't think you should get that close and put yourself at risk."

"No police. Please. I don't want to take a chance that something happens to Bella. After we have her back, you can call whoever you want to expose these guys. I promise to do whatever you tell me to do, but you have to let me help."

Damien shook his head. "I don't like it, but I know you well enough to understand your need to control this. If I have your promise, I'll do this your way. But at the first sign of trouble, all bets are off. And when it's time to make a move, you've got to let me handle every aspect of the situation first. To make sure it's all clear."

"I promise."

Damien looked like he wanted to say something else, but he turned away and headed for the kitchen. Lissa followed, noticing he already had his computer set up. He typed in several commands on the black screen, bringing it to life as the information loaded. It scrolled through, and line after line flashed before her eyes, the words meaning nothing to her. She'd never been a computer geek, but Damien clearly knew his way around the black hole of cyber-space.

And then everything stopped.

"This should work." He picked up his phone, pressed a few keys, and hit send. He glanced at her and smiled. "I just need someone on the SDS side to get me a secure code, and we'll be able to test this."

"Great." Lissa rocked back and forth, praying over and over for this locator system to work.

"Hey, Jason, it's Damien. I'm working on a case at a private residence. There's been an-other dognapping, and I'm trying to locate the dog. I put a chip in the collar this morning, and I've got the program loaded, but I need you to get me a response connect code with our secure-link system." She could hear the oth-er man on the line but couldn't make out his words.

"Here's the code on my end. Z14L6281Z. I'll hold while you get the response code."

Lissa didn't like him telling the guy at his office about what they were doing, but it didn't appear she had a choice in the matter. She just hoped he knew what he was doing and knew the people he worked with well enough to trust them. Trust had never come easily to her, but she was trusting Damien.

Several minutes later, she watched as he typed in the code.

"It seems to be working. Thanks." He hung up, looked at her, and nodded toward the screen.

"We're in."

Lissa leaned down next to him, her hair falling across his shoulder. She reached out to pull it back and hold it off to the side of her face. "Sorry." He smelled good this close, and it served as a reminder of when she'd thrown herself in his arms. And said she loved him.

"It's fine. I've always loved your hair." Damien looked at her, the same strange expression on his face from moments ago.

Something was on his mind, and she'd give anything to know what he was thinking. "What?"

"You know what I mean. You have nice hair. That's all I'm saying." Damien shrugged and turned back to the screen. Discussion over.

"So, what are we looking for?" She peered at the screen, making as much sense of the grid lines and markings as she did with Damien's unreadable expressions.

He reached for his wallet and pulled out a slip of paper. "As soon as I enter this chip number, we wait. The chip emits signals, and if it hits some of the cell towers nearby, it will send us the coordinates of where it pings. We can narrow down the area within a block or two with any luck. And then it's up to us to try to figure out exactly where they are holding her. Sometimes, we get lucky and get multiple pings we can triangulate into a better pinpoint area."

"Makes sense."

She watched as he typed in the chip number. They both waited for any sign of activity, Lissa barely breathing.

Nothing. No beep. No ping. No flashing marker. Nothing. She let out a frustrated sigh and straightened. "Now what?"

"We wait. Unfortunately, this is a huge city, and we don't have much to go on. You need to understand, there are lots of concrete walls and high buildings that interfere with the chip's signal. But if Bella is moved or relocated, we stand a better chance. Think of it as a cell phone. When you can't get reception, you move to different parts of a house or an area to get a signal. It's a lot like that. If she's still got that collar on, she's going to be in a location that we can alert."

"I'm not sure I can sit here and do nothing. That's not my style."

"We're not going to be doing nothing. While we wait, I'm going to find the best shot of your imposter this morning and see if we can't send it in for facial-recognition screening."

"That's a great idea. I hope we find this woman and put her behind bars where she belongs." Lissa paced in the kitchen while she listened for an alert from the computer. Damien was focused on reviewing the video footage, giving her a moment to watch him unnoticed.

I love you. Lissa still couldn't believe she'd blurted out her deepest secret. To Damien. It didn't get any worse. At least he thought her motivation was from an entirely different source. Gratitude versus honesty.

"Is this the woman?" he asked suddenly.

A quick glance was all it took for her to know.

"Yes." Lissa hissed the word as her lips tightened. Seeing the woman's face again brought it all back. Bella had reserved judgment for the woman when she'd first arrived, and it was unfortunate Lissa hadn't paid closer attention.

Damien reached out and grabbed her hand.

"We'll get her back. I promise."

The warmth of his hand gave her an ounce of comfort. It felt good to know someone was on her side, and that he cared. But then she'd thought he cared once before, and he'd proven her wrong.

She'd always wanted to ask him what happened between them. Years later, his decision not to ask her to prom still didn't make sense.

Just because her parents had become famous, didn't have a thing to do with them. In Lissa's mind, the prom would have been the official crossing over in their relation- ship. From friends to more than friends. To a couple.

"Damien, can I ask you something?" She withdrew her hand from his and took two steps back, folding her arms over her chest like a shield. Lissa swallowed hard when he stopped what he was doing to look up her.

"What is it?" His dark-brown eyes gazed at her with an intensity she found hard to bear without spilling her soul.

"I've always wanted to know—" A sudden loud beep came from the computer. *Bella?*

Lissa rushed back to Damien's side, her question forgotten. Adrenaline raced through her veins, her heart beating fast.

"Look." Damien pointed at one of the tiny grid marks on the screen.

"Is it her?"

"There's always the possibility of false signals, but it's unusual." He tapped on the screen and enlarged the map. "The signal is coming from the vicinity of Frazier and James Avenue. That's the far southeast section of town, close to the South Carolina border."

"Let's go. We can take my car."

"Your car is too obvious. My jeep will blend in better. We need to pack some food and blankets."

"Why? This isn't a picnic. We need to go get her."

"I told you this is a vicinity. We need to scout out the area, looking for the most likely places that a dog or dogs would be hidden. Rough looking houses, places with high fences, abandoned buildings. That sort of thing. We will know more once we get there. And then, if we can narrow it down, we sit and watch and wait. Unless you're looking to get hurt, you can't go busting into a place not knowing what to expect. We watch and move in when we know it's clear, or if an emergency presents itself and we're left with no choice." He cupped her face, his touch gentle yet commanding her to listen. "You promised me."

"I don't know how you do this. I'm not a patient person." She smiled, raising her hand to his. She needed to be careful before she found herself nursing another broken heart.

Damien stood and smiled. "Considering the racetrack is more your speed, I doubt you'd be patient in any other career." He bumped shoulders with her. It was the same thing he used to do when they were younger, back before he'd done the unforgivable and ditched her.

Chapter Nine

♥

OPENING THE PASSENGER DOOR of the jeep for Lissa, Damien helped her climb inside. "Ever the gentleman, I see." She flashed him one of her sweet smiles. The kind that made him long for the days when they were a lot closer—before fame and fortune had changed the girl he loved.

"I try." He went around the vehicle and hopped in, adjusting his jacket as he put on his seatbelt.

Lissa's gaze drifted downward, her eyes darkening when she noticed his gun. "I didn't realize you carried?"

"Always." He shrugged. At first, he'd been self- conscious of it strapped to his side, now he hardly remembered it was there.

"I never thought of investigating computer hacking as being a dangerous job," Lissa said, a worried frown on her face.

"If the computer hacking involves millions of dollars, it is. I'm not normally hired to handle email hacking." He shot her a smile, trying to ease her fears. "I've never had to use it, but it's a good precaution to have."

"Let's hope your track record continues. For Bella's sake," she corrected.

It would've been nice if her protectiveness extended to him, but he would be a fool to expect anything else from Lissa. "Were only about twenty minutes away from the general location. We need to go over the game plan before we get there." Having Lissa on the scene still made him uncomfortable, but she was the client, and for that reason alone, he would let her tag along if she followed his orders.

"You're the boss, and I did promise. *I* keep my promises."

There was something in the way she said the last sentence that gave him a feeling she was talking about far more than the stakeout. What, he wasn't sure. "Great. First, we sit tight and watch. This part is the hardest. We must narrow down where Bella is being held without alerting anyone else to what we're doing. This can take a while, which is why we brought food and water. Second, once we figure out where she's being held, we have to case the place to find out who's inside. We can't just go barreling in there and demanding Bella."

"I'm listening. But for the record, I don't agree. What if they are hurting her? And I know she's scared, so the sooner we get her out of there, the better." Lissa leaned against the passenger door, glaring at him, her lips a tight line of defiance.

"If we move in too quickly, they might panic and hurt her. I'd like to go the more thorough route and avoid a nasty surprise for the safety of all concerned." If they weren't on the same page, this could go horribly wrong. Maybe he should turn back now and take her home. It was the safest option. The last thing he wanted to do was put Lissa in danger.

"Fine." She took a deep breath and relaxed, surprising him with her easy acceptance. "So, what do we do until then?"

"I'm going to drive around twice and scope out the area. We can try to pinpoint locations that might be more favorable for holding a few dogs. Then we can park down the street to watch for anyone coming and going. Going, of course, would be the better option." Damien smiled. He'd already agreed to this insanity, taking it away without reason wouldn't be fair. Less troublesome, but not fair.

He drove around the block, pointing out a few of the older, rundown buildings. After narrowing it down to the two most likely possibilities, he parked the car. Luckily, both places could be seen from the corner of the side street where he parked.

"Now we wait." He turned off the engine and adjusted the seat back to recline more. "Keep your eyes peeled for any unusual activity."

"But it's getting dark, and it's going to be hard to see." Lissa removed her seat belt and settled back, following his lead.

"That's true. But it also means anyone moving about will need light. If you see any dancing lightning bugs, make sure you point them out." Damien chuckled.

"I didn't know we were on a nature expedition."

"We're not. This is the wrong time of year for lightning bugs. But it's a great way to spot people moving about. Cigarettes. Cell phones. Watch lights. Flashlights. Candles."

"I get the point."

Five minutes passed, and neither one spoke. The awkward silence prompted Damien to reach over to rub her shoulder. "It'll be okay." His attempt to reassure awakened more memories and he pulled his hand away, unwilling to give his brain free rein with his emotions. Thinking of the past would do nothing to help him solve this case. "Typically, in situations like this, the criminals might lay low for a few days, fully expecting the law to be hot on their heels looking for them. Especially in the case of Bella."

"Why especially Bella? Because she's a corgi?"

'No. Because she belongs to you." Lissa's sudden intake of breath made him realize she hadn't considered the possibility.

"You don't think…"

"I'm not making any assumptions, just speculating. But I will say this, not calling the police will be a surprise to whoever's got Bella. It might even make them jumpy."

Most of the other dogs taken had been purebreds, but none of them owned by a high-profile figure like Lissa, and no ransom notes had shown up. Damien had done his research and agreed the police weren't doing much to solve the case, something he intended to discuss with his friend at the station first chance he got. So far, the dognapper's motive was unclear.

"Does that mean you agree it was a good idea not to tell them?"

"Maybe, but it's highly unconventional. It's going to be a long night. I know we've had our differences in the past, but we're older now.

Maybe we can put those differences aside until Bella is found."

"It would make things easier. We could talk to pass the time."

Lissa's tentative acceptance of his olive branch surprised him, and he had no intention of letting it go to waste. "I'd like that. Last night, you mentioned you went to Kent State but then started racing. What happened? I always thought you watched with me just to hang out, not that you were really interested."

"Shows how little you knew me. I liked hanging out with you, but I loved the thrill of watching the drivers take control and race around the track at high speeds, destiny in their hands." The excitement in her voice spoke volumes about the love she still had for racing. It was in her blood.

He would do well to remember not to get to close to her again. Their futures were mapped out, and there was no direct route to connect them. "It's a good thing the second part didn't change."

"What's that supposed to mean?"

"The racing world wouldn't be the same if you hadn't put your mark on it. A lot more women are starting to get into the game now, because of women like you and the handful of others before you who paved the way." He admired her courage and wasn't afraid to tell her the truth.

"Thanks. That means a lot to hear you say that. But why did you specify the *second part* in your answer? Are you implying the part about liking to hang out with you changing was in any way my fault?"

Even in the darkness, he could feel the intensity of her gaze on him. "Nothing. It's all in the past. You're supposed to be watching for activity, not glaring at me." He shrugged.

"Suit yourself." Lissa retreated to the farthest corner of the passenger side, pressed up against the door.

So much for the truce between them. "I wasn't trying to upset you. Please, tell me more about college and the racing circuit. I find it all fascinating."

Lissa let out a deep breath. "Things were tough in college. After a few eye-opening experiences, I realized I didn't want to work for my parents. I wanted to make my own name in the world, and so I followed my passion for racing. I love the control out on the track, and the freedom it has given me off the track." The passion was back in her voice, her love for racing the one thing guaranteed to make her happy.

"Do you mean the freedom you have because of your financial success?"

"There's that. But it's more. I'm my own person. I control my own life and all aspects of it. For the most part, that means shutting people out. It's easier to maintain control that way. No surprises."

"That doesn't sound good. In fact, it sounds lonely." He never saw her as a keeping-people-out person. In fact, it was the exact opposite of the very public life she led.

"I've got Bella. That's why it's important for me to get her back. She and I understand each other."

"But what about love?" He couldn't keep from asking, although why he wasn't ready to analyze. "Surely there is someone special in your life. Or at some point, there will be. You're a beautiful woman who deserves to be loved." *Shut up, Trent.* It was like striking a match to a puddle of gasoline. A change in subject was in order.

"There is no one special, and I don't have to change the way I do things. It's my life, and I'm in control. Why change anything if I'm happy the way I am?"

"If you say so." He was happy to hear there was no man in her life and doubly excited to hear there were no prospective boyfriends were waiting in the wings. Not that he wanted to enter that race himself. They'd already passed their finish line, and he'd been the loser.

"What about you? You've been on a few dates lately. Does this mean you've got a happily ever after in sight, and now you want everyone else to have one, too?" Her voice had dropped to a low whisper.

Her perfume held hints of citrus and something else, he couldn't quite figure out, and the fragrant, alluring scent was wreaking havoc with his brain. "Hardly. I know we've had our differences, but I've always wanted you to be happy. That's never changed." It was the truth.

They might be on different life paths, but in his heart, she'd always be the young girl he remembered. The girl who was shy and sweet and wanted nothing more than someone to believe in her. He still believed in her, but she didn't need him as part of her fan club cheering her on—she already had plenty of those.

"How do you expect me to believe that?" Lissa turned away as she spoke, the back side of her barely visible.

"It's not about whether you believe it or not. It's the truth. I'm not the one who changed."

"You keep talking about changing, but I'm not the one who broke the promise you made me. I'm the one who was left hanging and wondering why you hated me so much." Her voice broke, making it sound as though she meant every word.

Clearly, they remembered differently. "I think your vision of the past has been clouded by your current success."

"And I think your vision of the past has been clouded by male stupidity," she snapped. Lissa had dropped the hurt from her voice like she'd flipped a light switch.

"You went from being a quiet, shy girl, to a showy, extrovert consumed with popularity. How do you not call that changing?"

"You don't know what it's like to be the wall-flower. To be the girl no one pays attention to. And then suddenly, my parents became a huge success, and everything changed. Their popularity spilled into my life, and I became popular. What girl in her right mind is going to reject the sudden attention? I was having fun, but it didn't change who I was inside. That girl was always the same and still is."

"I liked the girl you were and didn't ask you to change." Damien shook his head, fighting back the nagging thoughts forcing their way to the forefront of his brain. What if she was telling the truth? What if...no, no, no. *Tony Carruthers.* No matter what Lissa said, she'd picked the quarterback over him.

"Yes, I know. You told Haley I was a spoiled little rich girl. I think those were your exact words. The ones you said right before you asked her to the prom. I never did understand why you paid attention to me in the first place. You were on the football team and had lots of girls chasing after you. Your true colors came out when you ditched me and took my best friend instead. Had that always been your goal? To get to her?" Lissa's voice quivered. It couldn't be faked. No one was that good of an actress.

"I don't have a clue what you're talking about. I asked Haley to prom because I overheard Tony asking you and I got mad. You two were mighty chummy at the time. Call it young and dumb, but I do know I would have never said such a thing about you."

"Maybe you should've stuck around and waited for the answer."

What was that supposed to mean? Lissa had gone to prom with the quarterback—undeniable proof.

"If I had asked you to prom, would you have said yes? Haley said you accepted Tony." The nagging doubt was back in full force, Damien almost afraid of her answer.

"*If* you had asked, I *would* have said yes. I accepted Tony's second offer, the one to think about going with him. Not to actually go."

Recriminations started chipping away at his heart. It would seem Haley had had her own agenda. "Well, I guess it worked out the way it was supposed to. You two were king and queen that year, and if I remember correctly, you were the belle of the prom. You laughed and danced like it was the best night of your life."

He remembered watching her, beautiful in her yellow satin and lace gown, her hair cascading down one side with soft ringlets. And he remembered wishing he'd been her partner. Lovely Lissa had haunted his dreams for months.

"I had fun. I'm not going to lie. I went from wallflower to prom queen in the space of a few weeks. What girl wouldn't have thought it a dream come true? Especially, since the guy who promised to ask me, never did. Don't worry though, Tony was a good second choice—at least for prom night. But once my blinders were ripped away regarding the whole situation—my parents, my new friends, my popularity—it didn't take long to wear thin."

Damien shook off the past, his attention entirely focused on what Lissa was saying and trying to make sense of it. "What do you mean?"

"You broke your promise to take me. Haley took great joy reveling in your attention, her own popularity on the rise as a result. Tony only wanted the benefit of hanging out with my parents. He wanted to get close to the creators of the biggest video game to hit the market in twenty years. I started to realize it wasn't me who was popular, but my parents. I was just the inside track that led to them." Her voice had grown distant, like she, too, was remembering the past and not liking what she saw.

"I had no idea. You'd changed so much, and I didn't like it. I'm sorry. I wish I'd seen through it all." Damien meant it. The past could have been so different between them. Unfortunately, it didn't change the future. They were still two very different people.

"Me, too. It's why—look! There's a light over there in front of that building." Gone was the melancholy, and in its place was excitement.

Damien glanced over to where she pointed, and sure enough, someone was on the front stoop smoking a cigarette, the familiar orange glow bobbing up and down with each puff. The tall, bulky figure stood there a few minutes before walking to the street corner, turning right and disappearing out of sight.

"Can we go look inside?" Lissa pressed the button to unlock the door.

He reached over to stop her from exiting the vehicle. "Not yet. We sit tight and watch a few minutes to make sure he's gone. This is where I need your help. Once we're certain he's gone, I'm going to go look around. I'll try to peek in the windows and see what I can find out. I need you to sit in the car and keep an eye on the other building and make sure nothing happens over there. If anyone comes back, send me a text. I'll have it on vibrate so you can alert me to incoming trouble."

"That doesn't sound like much fun. I'd rather go with you and look for Bella."

Damien wasn't about to give in to the pleading in her voice. "But staying here is more important. Not to mention safer. Besides, you promised."

"Fine."

He was satisfied with her agreement, no matter how unwillingly given. Damien leaned over and dropped a kiss on her cheek. "It'll be fine. I promise." Kissing her felt natural and right. Maybe not the best idea given the circumstance, but it was too late to take it back.

He slid out of the car and crossed the street. Damien looked around, relieved no one was in sight. Pressing himself up against the large warehouse building, he edged his way to the first corner window. There were no lights on in the room, but the full moon gave him the ability to see what he needed to. There was no sign of anyone inside. He continued to move around the building's perimeter to check out the area and the other windows. Four in total, none of which netted him anything of use in his quest to find Bella.

It was almost disappointing because no activity more than likely meant this was the wrong location. Lissa would be upset to discover this was a dead end and adding to her grief over the situation was not something he wanted to do.

Damien tested the back door and was surprised to find it unlocked. At least it wasn't breaking and entering, just trespassing—and it was for a good cause. Not that he planned on getting caught. And if he did, he was banking on some of the friendships he cultivated over the years with the police force in town, to come in handy.

Gun in hand, he used the barrel to push the door open slowly, the creaking sound like crickets in the stillness of the night. He only opened it far enough to slip inside and press himself up against the wall to peered around, letting his eyes adjust to the darkness.

He hadn't taken but a couple of steps when he heard a sound behind him. Damien swung back, prepared for the worst.

"Damien?" The barest hint of a whisper floated down the hall.

Lissa.

He let out a sigh of relief and lowered his gun. "What are you doing here? I told you to wait in the car," he hissed.

"I didn't want either one of our phones to light up the darkness if I tried to text you, and I needed to let you know a van just sped away from behind the other house we were watching."

"Okay. Good thinking. Since it doesn't appear anyone is here, I'll check out the other place. Any chance I can get you to go back to the car and wait? If we get caught, it will better if you weren't inside with me." Damien knew the chances were slim to none, but it was worth a try.

"You can ask, but the answer will be no. Come on, let's go. Think of us like a Tracy-Hepburn duo. I can watch your back."

Damien groaned. "That's what I'm worried about. Because then who's watching yours?"

"I'll be fine. I've got you and your handy gun as my big, bad protectors."

"None of which is any use if you're behind me."

They crept down the alley that led to the other abandoned building. The sound of dogs barking could be heard even before they reached the back door.

"Do you hear that?" Lissa grabbed his arm, her voice unable to hide the excitement.

"I do. It's a good sign we are the right location this time. This is dangerous, Lissa. Are you sure I can't talk you out of coming in?"

"Not a chance, mister."

"Okay, then. Just follow my lead. The dogs will help cover any sounds we make but try not to talk once we are inside."

"Sure thing. Do you think anyone stayed behind to watch the dogs?"

"More than likely. But if it's one on one, we would have the element of surprise."

"Two on one."

"Lissa, you're here to calm Bella. Please stay away from anyone we come across and let me handle it."

"Come on, let's go." Lissa reached for the doorknob, discovering it locked.

Damien pulled the jackknife from his back pocket and made short work of the lock. So much for a simple trespassing charge—the stakes went higher the minute they entered the house. It wasn't the first time he'd had to do something like this in his line of work, and it probably wouldn't be the last.

Lissa started through the door, leaving him no choice but to follow. She was already taking control, even after her promise to follow his lead.

Stubborn woman.

Chapter Ten

♥

LISSA LET DAMIEN GO in front of her, remembering her promise. She followed him, imitating his movement as he kept close to the wall, avoiding any shafts of light coming through the windows.

The loud thumping of her heart felt like elephants on her chest. She understood the dangers, but she also understood that her baby might be just around the corner, or the next corner, or the next. It was enough to keep her moving forward.

Adrenaline coursed through her body, much like it did when she got behind the wheel of her racecar. Every time she strapped on her helmet and left pit road for the track, there was danger, but she'd learned to push fear away, just like she would do now.

The living room was empty, but the noise from the barking dogs grew louder. It came from up the stairs, and Damien waved his gun toward them to indicate they were going up. He pointed to her feet and then laid his finger across his lips, reminding her to be quiet.

Step by step, they made their way up. He held up his hand, cautioning her to stop.

Pressed up close to the first door, he listened and then nodded his head. He pushed open the door, glanced inside, and shook his head again before motioning for her to follow him.

He pointed at the door that led to the room where the barking was coming from. Lissa stayed close on his heels as he passed by the room and moved further down the hall.

She didn't dare ask questions and did exactly as he wanted, trusting his judgment. It had been a long time since she let someone control her decisions, but she also knew he was doing what he thought best for her and Bella.

Damien glanced in the next bedroom and continued checking all the other rooms on the second floor before making his way back to the dog room. He pressed his ear against the door and then reached for the handle.

Lissa found it hard to breathe.

Gun drawn and ready for action, Damien looked back at her, his steely gaze filled with warning. She nodded her head in understanding.

He flung open the door and stepped inside, his gun pointed as he scanned the room.

"Flip on the light, Lissa. There's no one here," he said, his voice low and commanding.

She let out the breath she hadn't realized she'd been holding. Lissa flipped the switch, and light filled the room. She blinked several times as she tried to adjust her eyes to the bright light.

When she looked around, her heart was filled with sadness as she took in cage after cage of kidnapped dogs. Her heart broke when as she realized there was no sign of Bella. She scanned the cages a second time, hoping she was wrong.

It didn't make any sense. She'd been so sure they were going to find Bella.

Only one cage stood empty, and as she moved closer, Lissa noticed the pink collar. Her heart lodged in her throat, choking her. She moved closer and picked up the collar. The heart-shaped tag's inscription delivered the final blow.

Bella. Lissa clutched the collar to her chest.

Damien had come to stand next to her. He pulled her against him, wrapping his arms around her. "I'm sorry. At least we know she was here. We won't stop looking, I promise."

"If only we'd come here first. Maybe Bella was in that van I saw pulling away." Tears rolled down her face unchecked.

"We don't know that, and either way, it won't change things now. We have to stay positive, for Bella's sake."

She nodded her head, finding it impossible to speak. She clung to Damien like a lifeline, needing his strength more than ever.

"I hate to say this, but we need to call the police. Finding these dogs changes everything.

We've got eleven dogs whose owners will be happy to get them back."

"Won't we get in trouble for being here?"

"Maybe, but I'm banking on calling in a few favors. I've got friends at the station."

"I understand. Do what you have to do."

"Don't forget, the police may be able to dust for prints or find other clues that will lead us to Bella. It's worth the risk." Lissa nodded, realizing the truth in what he said.

Damien walked away to make the call, leaving her to feel more alone than she would have thought possible. She hadn't been dependent on anyone in years, but it seemed that ever since Damien kissed her, the walls surrounding her heart had come tumbling down. She needed him in a way she'd never needed anyone before, and it was scary.

One by one, she opened each cage to pet the dogs, reassuring them all was well. Doggy licks were her reward for rescuing these animals, and it brought her in some small way, a level of joy to know these dogs would have happy endings.

Damien was right. Going after Bella didn't stop here. This was just a curve in the track. "Why do you think they took her and left the others?" Based on the one-dog-per-cage setup in the room, it bothered her to think Bella was the only one missing from the stolen dogs.

"I'm not sure." Damien's hesitation before he answered made her glance harder at him.

Did he know more than he was telling? She wanted to ask but for some reason held her tongue.

It didn't take long before sirens filled the air as the police cars pulled up in front of the house, the flashing lights illuminated on the windows of the bedroom.

Damien went downstairs to greet the officers. She heard their footsteps on the stairs right before the room suddenly filled with uniformed police officers.

"Miss Walker, Mr. Trent has filled us in on what's going on. Not smart breaking and entering a house and taking the law into your own hands. Good thing for you your boyfriend has connections. I don't agree with not hauling you both down to the station, but I'm not the one calling the shots. I need a description of your missing dog." The tall officer stood imposingly close, and Lissa took a step back.

"He's not my boyfriend, and I just wanted my dog back. If you have a pet of your own, surely you can find a way to understand. My dog is a corgi. Short legs, long body. Short fur. White, black and tan. Her name is Bella, but her collar was left here." She held it up to show the man.

"I see. Any reason you didn't report your dog missing when it first happened?" He stopped writing to look up at her from his notebook.

Officer Brown wasn't happy, but she didn't care. She'd do the same thing over again given a chance. "There's been a lot of dognapping and not a lot of arrests. I just thought it better to snoop around on my own. Any report you took would have just been added to the file with all the other non-urgent cases."

His scowl deepened. "That's not your call to make. If a crime is committed, you need to report it, whether you agree with our methods or not. We have a lot of cases, and it's not easy to designate a task force for a dognapping ring."

Blah. Blah. Blah. Tell it to someone who believes you.

"How did you managed to find these dogs?" The man was using his interrogation voice, and it rattled Lissa.

She didn't like being questioned like she was the criminal. Who cared how they found them? It was an old house, and by the looks of it, no one lived here. They should be happy the dogs had been found and that they could close eleven dognapping cases. It was more than the police had managed to do in the past few weeks.

"Damien put a tracker on Bella's collar."

"The non-boyfriend. So, what is your relationship status?"

"Damien is with SDS, a security company I hired to guard Bella until someone put a stop to the dognappers. I actually hired Travis Howard, but he had a family emergency, and Damien had to step in at the last minute." She let out a deep breath, trying to keep calm.

"So where was Damien when Bella was stolen?" Why would he suspect Damien? But then again, he had a funny look on his face earlier when she'd asked him about why someone would have taken Bella away from this place. She'd wondered then if he knew more than he was letting on.

"On a date to the best of my knowledge. Not where I thought he should've been, but that's another story." And not something she wanted to make public knowledge so the media could paint her as some jealous ex-girlfriend. They would if they knew her and Damien's history. Whether it was true or not didn't matter—it would make good headlines.

"Interesting." She followed the officer's gaze and found him watching Damien across the room.

She turned back to the officer. "What is?"

"It's just that you hire a new security guy who's not there to do his job, and then suddenly your dog is stolen. The classic case of an inside job." The officer *did* think Damien had something to do with it. Damien may have a few friends at the station, but this guy wasn't one of them.

"Do you have insurance on Bella?" Officer Brown asked.

"What kind of question is that? Are you hinting that I had something to do with her disappearance?" First, he was implicating Damien, and now her.

"I'm not hinting at anything. I'm just asking the questions."

"Well, I don't like the question. The answer is no.

No insurance. Be sure to write that down in your little notebook in big capital letters. Bella is a member of my family."

The officer closed his notebook. "I'm not trying to be a jerk. These are reasonable questions. One last thing, any reason someone might have a vendetta against you?"

Lissa let out a dry laugh and shook her head. "Only every guy I beat out on the racetrack."

"I thought you looked familiar, but I didn't put two and two together. Sorry. We will do everything we can to find your dog. Can you stick around for a bit? I want to ask Mr. Trent a few questions before you leave."

"Sure." Lissa hated to admit it, but she wanted to hear whatever Damien had to say.

The detective went over to talk to Damien, and Lissa edged closer, kneeling to pet one of the dogs close enough to hear what was said.

"Mr. Trent, I know you're the one who called us, and I know Captain Miller and Sargent Jackson have vouched for you, but I still have my job to do, and that means asking you a few questions."

"Ask away. I'll take all the help I can get to reunite Lissa and Bella."

"I understand from Miss Walker you were recently hired to watch her dog. She also mentioned you were filling in for another employee by the name of Travis Howard."

Damien shrugged. "Yes, that's correct."

"It's my understanding you were away on a date of some sort when Bella was stolen from her residence. Do you have any proof of your whereabouts?"

Damien bristled at the officer's implication. "You can't be serious? Are you putting me on your list of suspects?" "Not yet. Just answer the question." Lissa leaned closer.

"It wasn't a date. I coach Little League on Thursday nights, and we have games on Saturdays. I take my responsibilities to the boys quite seriously, and this job was sort of sprung on me. You should have no problem verifying my story." Damien searched the room, his furious gaze landing on her.

Little League. How was she supposed to know? All he'd had to do was tell her the truth. She'd wronged Damien with her false accusations, but it was partly his fault.

The officer seemed satisfied with Damien's explanation and jotted down a few notes. "Thanks. You know I had to ask. I'm just doing my job."

"I know. I know." The tension had left Damien's voice, and his stance was more relaxed.

"What I'm trying to figure out though, is why only Miss Walker's dog was taken when whoever was here split earlier? Any suggestions?"

"It's Lissa Walker. My first guess would be money." Damien shrugged.

She knew deep down that Damien was right, this was about money. It was just a matter of time, and she'd hear from someone. She'd pay, and then Bella would be home. It was the only way Lissa could deal with what was happening and remain positive as to the outcome.

"I admit that's a distinct possibility, but it still doesn't make any sense why they have all these other dogs and have done nothing with them. And another question, Miss Walker mentioned you put a chip on the dog's collar. According to her statement, these people left in a rush. Who else knew that you and Miss Walker were staking out the place tonight? Something had to have tipped them off that you were here."

She hadn't thought of that, the source of her distrust becoming front and center. How *did* the bad guys know? It was a question she wanted answered.

Was it a coincidence? Or was Damien in some way involved? Just because he had an alibi for his whereabouts didn't totally rule him out. She wanted to believe he had nothing to do with it, especially after the kiss he'd dropped on her cheek back in the car. That had been a kiss of care and concern. *But what if she was wrong?*

"I've been wondering that myself. On both accounts. But unfortunately, I don't have any viable answers yet." Damien appeared deeply concerned, but that didn't mean a thing.

"If you find out anything, be sure to let me know."

"Will do." The two men shook hands, and the officer went to help the others round up the dogs.

From now on, she'd be paying close attention to Mr. Trent. Whether from old feelings reignited, or because she wanted to discover the truth of Bella's whereabouts and thought he might be part of the answer, she didn't know.

Chapter Eleven

♥

THE RIDE HOME HAD been quiet, unlike the time spent together during the stakeout. Damien hadn't liked the detective's implications and hoped the man hadn't shared his views with Lissa, but he didn't hold out much hope for wishful thinking. She'd been crouched nearby, well within hearing range. And he'd seen the tension written clearly in her expression.

Something had changed between them during the stakeout. The renewed connection was undeniable. It was as if the years they'd spent apart had vanished, although he wasn't sure it was a good thing. All the reasons he'd walked away in high school still existed. And yet he hadn't been able to stop himself from kissing her cheek. All in the name of comfort, of course.

She'd blamed her silence during the ride home on disappointment, and he'd been all too happy to give her space. It had given him a chance to think things through as well, without having to make small talk.

This morning and today would be another story. They needed to regroup and figure out a new game plan. It wasn't just doing a job successfully that drove him to action, it was also Lissa's happiness. He hated to see the light of joy extinguished in her eyes, and he wanted to be the one to put it back. To bring Bella home.

He grabbed the newspaper off the front porch and headed for the kitchen. After pouring a cup of coffee, he settled in at the table for his morning ritual. Damien unfolded the paper, the headline immediately grabbing his attention.

Dognapper Strikes Again but Eleven Stolen Dogs Found.

There was a photo of Lissa and Bella, and then one of him and Bella at the track yesterday. Damien shook his head, unhappy with the turn of events. He hated publicity, not only because of what happened with his parents and the media, but also because in his line of work, the fewer who knew the truth about what he did, the easier it was to do his job. And now he'd been thrown right into the middle of it. He should have known reconnecting with Lissa Walker would bring the wrong kind of attention.

The article went into great lengths to proclaim them as heroes for discovering the whereabouts of the other dogs, and there was much speculation as to the relation- ship between Lissa and her new doggy guard.

He hated that phrase.

Lissa came into the kitchen fully dressed, her hair and makeup were perfectly done. She wasn't usually a morning person, leaving him to wonder where she was headed. Staying one step ahead of her was difficult at best.

"Good morning." She poured a cup of coffee and took a long sip.

"Morning. Going somewhere?"

"No. I have lots to do today, starting with a press appointment at eight. You should be prepared." She gave him the once over. "Do you have anything a little less He-Man?"

He-Man? His T-shirt and jeans were good enough for him, and he couldn't care a less about the media.

"How did that come about? I thought you were after more privacy?" This was the crux of the problem between them. She would always be in the limelight. It was a part of who she was.

"I do. But sometimes things happen that take you out of your comfort zone. I love Bella, and I will do anything to help bring her home. *Anything.*"

"Count me out. Not my deal. And I prefer you to keep SDS out of your conversation with the press. It's a security company, and a little discretion goes a long way."

"Suit yourself. It's just an official statement for a press release. I want to spread the word and put pictures of Bella out in the world. Maybe someone will see her and call the hotline I'm setting up. I also want to make it hard for whoever's behind this to get away with what he's done."

"I get it. It's a good idea." Hotlines were useful, but every corgi out there would probably merit a call, people hoping they spotted Bella and could cash in on the reward. It would mean extra manpower on the phone line, but it was worth a try. He didn't have a whole lot of better ideas.

"Will you be at the Coca-Cola 600 cocktail party tonight with me? It was on the original schedule." "I'm not sure there's a reason, all things considered." Lissa looked hurt, his callous words a reminder of the circumstances. He should be there to support her. "I'll go if you want me there."

She nodded, shooting him a soft smile to show her she was pleased with his answer. "Thanks. I'd like that." The doorbell rang. The lack of answering bark from Bella magnified the hole her absence made.

Lissa left to answer the door, returning moments later with by a few reporters and cameramen. Damien stood off to the side to watch the proceedings, his distaste for the media evident in the tension holding his body as tight as guitar strings. One over- the-top pluck and he'd snap.

Lissa retrieved a photo of Bella off the mantel and took her place as the others gathered around. It was only as she started to make a statement that he realized he hadn't shown her the newspaper this morning. He hadn't warned her about the direction the media had taken their relationship.

There was nothing he could do to stop the fallout but watch and wait. He hoped he was wrong, but his experience with journalists had taught him well. The worst would always come, and they didn't care who they hurt if they got their story. Lissa's words faded into a blur as Damien recalled the run-in with his parents and the media.

"What's the story between you and Damien? Is he more than your doggy guard?" The reporter's question pulled him from his miserable walk down memory lane.

"What do you mean? He's a friend if that's what you're asking." Lissa answered smoothly, not at all flustered by the direction the conversation was going.

"Where was he when Bella was taken?" The journalist zeroed in with deadly accuracy on the same issue the officer had presented.

Damien was getting tired of everyone automatically thinking he might have something to do with Bella's disappearance.

Lissa glanced at him, for the first time looking unsure of herself. "He was at a Little-League game."

She knew. And could have only found out last night when the detective had started asking questions, confirming she'd overheard the conversation.

"Sounds like a reasonable alibi." The reporter laughed. "I understand you two were friends in high school. What happened? You two haven't been linked at all since you've been racing."

"My private life is none of your business. You agreed to stay focused on Bella's disappearance in exchange for this interview. Stay on point, or we're done here." She handled them expertly, like she'd done it a million times.

Damien's respect for her rose another notch. The interview lasted no more than another ten minutes, and then the flurry of activity ceased, and they were gone. He pushed off from the wall and headed to the kitchen.

Minutes later, Lissa joined him.

"I'm glad that's over. I hope someone sees or hears something and we get a good lead." She poured a fresh cup of coffee and leaned up against the counter.

"I don't know how you do it, but you sure know how to handle them." Damien loved the way her hair fell on either side of her face, the curls bouncing lightly as she moved. She was fresh and beautiful. It was no wonder the media loved her despite the Maneater nickname.

"You have good reason to distrust them, but sometimes, like now, they can be beneficial." Lissa blew on the coffee and then took a sip.

"The media and I have a long-standing hate relationship. They can keep their benefits."

Lissa crossed the room and laid a hand on his arm. "Didn't you say your parents are better now after all that happened? Try to focus on the positive that came from the ordeal."

"It's kind of hard when anytime you search the internet for Jack Trent, the first thing you find is article after article about the embezzlement charges. It never goes away. And the tiny retraction with the truth doesn't show up until you get through about twenty pages of lies." His conditioned response spilled out, hoping to put an end to her interest.

She dropped her hand and stepped away. "I don't need to search. None of that matters. I understand the media all too well. For me, it's a part of what I must do. It's all for a good cause." That's where the two of them were so different. Her cause was fame and fortune—two things that didn't matter to him.

"Your cause perhaps, not mine. You're welcome to them." His beef was with the media, not her, but he wasn't sure how to turn off the automated responses he'd honed over the years.

"Thanks for helping me to understand the situation better. I like that we can talk." Lissa smiled. "And I like you, too. As much as I didn't want to work with you, I'm glad you're here to help me through this."

"Even though I wasn't here when the dognapper struck?" They'd gone from not friends to mutual admiration, and it felt right.

"Yes. Even though you weren't here. How can I be mad at you for not disappointing the Little League kids?" Lissa chuckled. It was nice to see her smile again, and even better to realize he had something to do with it.

"So you heard that?" he asked.

"Yes. Wish you would have just told me."

"And miss the hint of jealousy you displayed when you thought it was an actual date? Never."

Lissa shook her head to the contrary, but he noticed she didn't deny it.

He wished things could be different between them, because somehow, the old feelings he'd once had were back, stronger than ever. Unfortunately, nothing had changed, and it would never work between them.

"We haven't talked about this yet, but the detective last night made me think of something. Is there anyone who would target you? Anyone who sees you as a real enemy?"

"He asked me the same thing. There's always lots of jealous people, Razor more so than others. You saw him in action the day before yesterday. But I don't think he's capable of dognapping, or that he would take his dislike of me to that level."

"I can't count out anyone. I'll do some digging around. Anyone else?"

"There are always people trying to get to my parents. But again, they don't have any new video games releasing, so there's nothing to go after except money. Taking Bella to make demands on my parents seems like a stretch." Lissa stared out the kitchen window into the backyard.

"I agree. I'll start looking into Razor and see what I can find out. Just to be on the safe side. What time is the cocktail party tonight?"

She turned back to face him, her eyes glassy with tears. "It starts at six. But I guess you don't need to go now—since you won't need to watch Bella," her voice barely audible as she finished the sentence.

"True. But I'd like to be there for you, and you never know, I might pick up some clues while I'm there." He wanted to help. Correction, he needed to help. And not because of the contract—but because it was Lissa.

"Thanks, but that won't be necessary." She shrugged.

She was shutting him out, but he wouldn't let her. Not now. "Lissa, I'll be there whether we drive in together or not. It was my job to watch Bella, and it's my job to get her back."

"Fine. We'll need to leave around five to get there in time."

"Okay. I'll redirect the hotline calls to someone at the office. That should take a load off you. Just try to relax today and see if you can think of anyone else who might be a suspect. I'm going to go investigate a few things, drive around the area, and head back over to where the dogs were being held. Maybe talk to some people to see what they saw. And I'll see if the detectives found any clues. You never know when or where we might get a lead." He crossed the room and took her in his arms, unable to resist trying to ease the sadness in her eyes and voice.

She laid her head against his chest, fitting perfectly. "Thanks. I appreciate your help. I'll meet you here tonight, and we can ride together."

Damien dropped a kiss on the top of her head.

She looked up at him, a question in her eyes. Her lips parted slightly, inviting him to kiss her.

Cinnamon. It was the scent he hadn't been able to identify before. Cinnamon and citrus. Dynamite combination for a dynamite woman. He wanted to respond to the invitation, and for once, he couldn't think of any reason not to give in.

As his lips met hers, the feeling of rightness only intensified. *Finally.* One of his biggest regrets in high school had been never kissing Lissa, but it was worth the wait.

The other regret was letting her go without a fight.

Chapter Twelve

♥

LISSA PULLED UP AT the Grand Hotel on Main street and waited in the valet line.

"Thanks for coming with me tonight, Damien." She forced a smile, but missing Bella made it difficult. Lissa would have blown off the cocktail party if it wasn't be held by the sponsors of next week's big race at the Charlotte Motor Speedway, her hometown racetrack.

"Glad to help. I can do some people watching and see if we get any leads."

She should have known the only reason he was here was to do his job. For a small window of time, she'd thought he was coming as her friend, which considering his kiss, was a reasonable assumption. She'd given herself over to the moment, and Damien's lips had almost seemed like a lifeline. But then he'd pulled away, stepped back, made some lame excuse and left. When would she learn?

She handed the valet her keys and got out of the car, coming around the front to meet up with Damien. They walked side by side up the stairs. Lissa's heel slipped on the top step, forcing her to grab Damien's arm for support. "Sorry."

"Don't be. I'm not." He smiled, sending her a mixed signal.

She started to pull her hand away, but he held it firmly in place. "Safer this way."

"It'll start rumors." Not to mention it would start her wishing for something that would never be.

"I'm afraid it's too late to worry about that based on recent headlines."

"True."

They made their way into the event room, and Damien dropped her arm but stayed close by. It gave her a sense of security and the strength she needed to get through this event, when what she really wanted to do was be out looking for Bella.

As she made the rounds and introduced Damien to everyone she knew, she could sense his distance.

He was cordial to a T, but that's where it stopped.

These people weren't the media, so she didn't understand the vibes radiating from him.

"What's wrong?" Lissa asked him as they waited in line for a drink at the bar.

"Nothing. Why?" He shrugged, turning away to observe the crowded room.

"I can tell you don't want to be here. I'm just trying to figure out why."

"You don't, either." He shot her a look that dared her to contradict his statement.

"True, but we know why I'm doing it. What about you? Is the only reason you're here for work?" She hated the vulnerability in her voice. Lissa needed the kiss to mean more. Wanted it to mean more.

"No. I'm starting to wonder if maybe letting our friendship go was a mistake." Damien watched her intently, his words taking her by surprise.

A flush of pleasure spread through her body, and she moved closer. "Maybe." It was no more than she'd been thinking. Any thought she had regarding his potential involvement in Bella's disappearance vanished.

He liked her, and she liked him. And once upon a time, she'd trusted him. She could do it again.

"Nice blush." He grinned.

"It's the wine." Lissa lied, not quite ready to admit the whole truth.

"If you say so. Maybe later, I'll put that theory to the test, because we're both know that kiss meant something." Damien dared to wink, making her feel like she was the only woman in the room.

The warm flush across her skin deepened, and she fanned herself with the drink coaster. "It's just hot in here. Don't go getting any ideas."

Damien chuckled and placed his arm around her side to draw her near possessively.

Two other drivers came over, ending the intimate moment. Lissa introduced Damien, and the conversation quickly ventured into shop talk.

"You looked good at your last practice. Think you'll make the pole?" Clark Jones was a great driver and not one of the men who took issue with her being on the track.

"Of course. I've been studying some videos and might have a few slick moves to try out." Lissa nudged Clark in the shoulder, teasing him.

Clark grinned and shook his head. "Did you hear that Winston's trying to get some newly designed tire approved? Claims the tread will hold up longer at the higher temps late in the race."

"Sounds promising. If he could handle the car on the turns better, maybe he wouldn't need them." Everyone laughed at her comment. Good-natured ribbing was always fun.

Damien excused himself and walked away.

Clearly, shop talk wasn't his thing.

"How's your wife doing, Charlie? I heard she's pregnant." Lissa turned to the man who recently won at Talladega.

"She's doing great other than some bouts of morning sickness. I'll tell her you asked about her. It'll make her day. She must root for me, but I swear she secretly cheers you on. She's a big fan of yours."

"That's so—"

"Well, if it isn't the Maneater. Guess you being here means you weren't smart enough to drop out of the 600." *Ugh.* She wasn't in the mood to deal with Razor so soon after their last encounter.

"Now why would I do that? I seem to remember I beat your time by eight minutes and fifty-three seconds last time we raced in Charlotte. If anyone should bow out, it should be you."

The others laughed, thinking it a typical rivalry, not fully aware of the undercurrent.

"You got lucky. It happens." Razor didn't let up.

"Is that how you managed to qualify? Luck?" She wasn't about to back down from the odious man, but she also had no intentions of sticking around to let the conversation get out of hand. "I've got to find Damien."

Lissa turned and walked off. She'd been here an hour, more than enough to make it official. Slipping away sounded like a great idea.

She spotted him off to one side of the room, his back to her. He was surrounded by three women dressed in sleek designer gowns, their hair and makeup perfect, their smiling painted lips laughing at something Damien said. The raised voices of the group reached her ears as she drew closer.

"You'd think she'd be out looking for her dog instead of racing. She doesn't belong on the race- track. It's a man's sport, and these women thinking they can compete just make a mock- ery of the skills needed to perform at such a high professional level." The woman's disdain dripped from her voice.

Lissa stopped in her tracks, partially hidden by a large palm plant. The insult brought back memories she didn't want.

Haley telling her Damien had called her a spoiled, rich girl, and then her friend going to prom with him. The women in her communications group at college talking in the library about how she was a little princess. That comment had wounded her to the core. She'd thought they were her friends, but she'd thought wrong. And then there was Jasper, her college boyfriend. It had come as a rude awakening to discover he was only interested in getting to know her parents. Once she'd found out, she'd promptly dumped him, but the lesson had still hurt.

The one good thing that had come from it all was it had given birth to her determination to make a life of her own. One she could control. One where she didn't need other people who could use her unless she was gaining something from the deal as well.

That was the day she'd decided to follow her dream and get into stock car racing. And she'd never looked back. Until now. The comment stung.

"I agree, women don't belong in racing. My George lost out last year getting to Daytona because of Lissa Walker, and then she got sent home after losing out at the pole. Wasn't fair at all." Of course, the woman hadn't considered George didn't make it because of his skills, not something she took from him.

Lissa's anger rocketed like a turbo engine on high-octane fuel, the result landing somewhere between *like to kill* and *not worth it*, but mostly on *like to kill*.

"Damien, you work with her. What's she like? Does the name fit?"

Lissa had started forward to give the group a piece of her mind, but stopped, determined to hear his answer. Her heart beat faster. It was hard to focus. To breathe. But she waited. She had to know the truth.

His back was to her, and she couldn't make out his words. Only bits and pieces drifted her way. But the women's laughter in response was all she needed to hear to know it wasn't good. He'd joined in the merriment at her expense. Just like the others back in high school and again in college.

Lissa closed her eyes and took several deep breaths. No good would come from confronting the group and making a scene, and there was no way she wanted to give the media any fodder. On top of everything with Bella, Damien's betrayal was simply too much. Her iron control was slipping fast. She stepped out onto the terrace to regroup.

The Maneater had manners, something those women had apparently never learned.

"Sorry to hear about Bella." A woman she recognized from the racing circuit stopped her.

"It's a devastating turn of events. Thanks."

"I hope you get her back. I read how you saved the other dogs. I can't imagine how you felt not finding her with them." Her comments made Lissa stop and take notice.

"It was awful, but I'm happy for the other owners." The woman continued to talk, unaware of the pain she was causing.

Lissa's stomach twisted another notch as she thought of Bella for the hundredth time that evening. She'd had more than enough. And as for Damien, he could find his own ride back to the house. Or walk for that matter. She wanted nothing more to do with him. "I've got to run. Thanks."

The woman eyed her strangely. Had her interest been purely compassion, or was there more to her comments? Lissa would have to ask around and get her name. Damien was making her suspicious of everyone.

"Okay. Take care."

Lissa spotted two of the hosts standing near the door. Perfect. She made her way over to them.

"Goodnight, and thanks. I've got to run. It's been a stressful day." Lissa shook hands with the men.

"I'm sure. We were sorry to hear about Bella. She's kind of fixture with you on the circuit. I hope you find her soon." Bill Evans had always been kind to her and supportive of her decision to compete on the track. Men like him were few and far between.

"Thanks. It's been tough."

"Will you still be doing the pole trials, or will you be pulling out of the race?" Darren, the other sponsor, asked.

"I'm racing. I'm strong enough to keep my personal life and my professional life separate. Don't worry." She regretted the harsh words the minute she said them. It wasn't his fault she was in a bad mood.

"I wasn't insinuating you couldn't." He looked apologetic.

"I'm sorry. I'm a bit off right now. I've got to go."

"Lissa, take care of yourself." Bill stepped closer and gave her a hug.

"Thanks." She stopped at the coat check to retrieve her wrap. As she turned to leave, a man approached her holding a silver platter.

"Miss? Wait. Are you Lissa Walker?" The man had a thin, wiry face, and his glasses were pushed back on the bridge of his nose as he peered at her.

"I am." *Now what?*

"I have a letter for you. A gentleman asked me to deliver this before you left."

"Thank you." Lissa took the letter and shrugged, unsure of who it could possibly be from. She tore open the seal as the man disappeared into the crowd. *Strange.*

She pulled out the paper and unfolded it, surprised to see the SDS logo at the top. She started to read the words and then stopped, their meaning sinking in after the first sentence.

I have something of yours.

Bring one million dollars in cash to 26 Maple Street at five pm on Friday. Cash only. Unmarked bills. Use a blue duffle bag and leave it on the kitchen table. Bella will be tied to the table and waiting. Come alone, or Bella pays for your mistake. I'll be watching, so don't try anything funny. You won't like the consequences.

A ransom note.

She sucked in a deep breath, forcing the air through her lungs, trying to breathe. This was all about money. Damien had suspected as much, and deep down, Lissa had thought the same.

She shook her head. It couldn't be Damien. No. No. No. She'd trusted him. A picture of him laughing with the women flashed before her eyes.

Mistaken trust. The letter was proof he was involved. *Wasn't it?* He was at Little League—or so he said. Maybe he was working in cahoots with someone else.

A million dollars. For Bella, she'd pay. *And Damien knew it.*

The emotions she'd been holding in check exploded. She rounded on the balls of her feet and made her way back into the room.

"Did you forget something, Lissa?" Bill looked up and asked as she approached.

"Sort of," she snapped, not slowing her pace in the slightest as she breezed past him.

Damien was at the bar, his gaze scanning the room in search of someone.

If he was her, he'd be wishing differently by the time she got through with him. She stormed across the room and tapped him on the shoulder.

He spun around. "There—"

"Don't talk, you rat." She held up the note. "You had something to do with Bella's disappearance, didn't you?" She couldn't control the rage or the volume of her voice.

"Hardly. What's this all about?" Damien's shocked expression registered, but it didn't change a thing.

"A ransom note. On a page with the SDS letterhead. So, it's either you, Travis, or someone you work with. I should have known better than to trust you. I. Want. Her. Back. Now." Lissa poked his chest with her finger to emphasize every word. She was past caring about the people gathering around. Past caring about the media snapping pictures.

"I don't have her. You've got this all wrong." Damien backed away, holding his hands up.

"I hired you to keep her safe, and SDS failed me. Now this!" She flung the note at him. "You're fired!"

She turned and marched out of the room, not stopping to talk to anyone. The tears threatening to spill over wouldn't stay put much longer, and there was no way she wanted to show any sign of weak- ness in a room full of her peers.

Nothing could have prepared Damien for the sudden change in Lissa or her very public accusation claiming he had something to do with Bella's disappearance. It proved how little she really knew him. The attraction between them would never be enough.

Her over-the-top response had the entire room at a standstill, and now, all eyes were on him to see what he would do. Except he wasn't about to give them what they wanted. More gossip for the rag papers and something to talk about for the next few weeks. Lissa had done an excellent job of that all on her own. The disdainful, haughty stares of the guests showed they believed Lissa's charge that he was somehow involved.

Without a word, he headed for the door. There was only one thing left he could do. Prove her wrong. Not only was the reputation of SDS at stake, but his own as well.

Chapter Thirteen

♥

THE PAST DAY AND a half dragged on endlessly for Lissa. She knew what she had to do, even if Bev thought she was crazy. As both her friend and her manager, she'd urged Lissa not to give in to the ransom demands, but there really wasn't any choice. The police hadn't found anything that would lead them to Bella and the dognappers, and she hadn't heard anything from Damien since the party. Not that she should. She and SDS were finished.

There was still the matter of his belongings. The next time Bev came by, she'd clean out his things and have her friend deliver them. If he wasn't behind bars by then.

Little League coach. She really didn't want to believe he was involved, but someone in his office was, and it was easier to make him the target with no other face to replace his.

If there were any other choice, she'd take it. But the dognapper had been clear. If anyone showed up with her at the drop, they'd kill Bella. She wasn't willing to risk it. The money she could replace, Bella she could not.

The bank had been the kink in the plan. That sum of money demanded wasn't available on such short notice. The manager assured her it would be possible by Monday, but that was too late. Lissa hoped the two hundred thousand she did get, would be enough to keep the dognapper happy. Better still, maybe the jerk wouldn't realize there was a shortage until after she and Bella were long gone.

She'd deal with the fallout after she had Bella back.

Lissa glanced at her watch. There wasn't much time left before she had to go. The note said three o'clock sharp. She typed a text to Bev and scheduled it for 3:15. That way, Lissa knew her friend would call the police if she hadn't heard from her by 3:45. It was Lissa's only assurance that backup would be on the way if anything went wrong.

Lissa dressed in dark jeans, a T-shirt, and pulled on a black sweatshirt. She didn't want to be recognized. The Porsche was a problem, but she wasn't the only person in town that owned one. Hopefully, this was a section of town where her car would at least be safe for the sixty seconds she planned on being in the building.

Get in. Get out. That was the game plan. Her hands shook as she grabbed her gun and holster from the dresser drawer where she kept it hidden. She'd only shot it at the range for practice. This would be the first time she'd be putting her concealed-carry license to use. She strapped the holster through her belt loops and adjusted it into place. After checking the gun to make sure it was loaded and the safety was on, she slid in the holster and snapped the strap over it to hold it in place.

Lissa pulled her sweatshirt down over it to keep it out of sight. No sense giving away all her secrets. She brushed her hair back into a ponytail and secured it out of her face. Big round sunglasses finish the image. *No one should recognize me now.*

She grabbed the keys from her purse, her gaze landing on the dark-blue duffel bag on the bed. It was a stark reminder of the danger she was heading into. She picked up the duffel bag and made her way downstairs and to the garage.

Adrenaline raced through her body. Her fingers twitched against the steering wheel. *Take a deep breath.*

Lissa backed out the garage and then put the car in gear, the engine revving as she stepped on the gas and headed to the drop-off point. Her stomach clenched, nausea making her wish she'd foregone even the piece of toast and coffee she'd had for breakfast. She arrived at the designated location ten minutes ahead of schedule to case the place. Mimic- king Damien, she cruised around the block once before parking. Lissa thought of their time together during the stakeout. He'd kissed her on the cheek like he cared. And then there was the other kiss.

Stop it. This was no time for memory lane, especially one that stung.

Lissa pulled up in front of the house. It was a small nondescript rundown track home, every house on the street a copy of each other except for the color. This house would have been white if not for the peeling paint and mold.

The place looked empty. No curtains on the windows. No furniture on the stoop. No yard art or anything else to indicate someone resided here. She glanced from side to side with each step she took. The bag lay heavily against the gun, the pressure against her side a reminder of both the danger and the protection she carried.

She knocked on the door, not really expecting anyone to answer. This wasn't a social call. Lissa strained to hear any sounds from inside. If Bella barked, at least Lissa would know this wasn't a setup.

Nothing but complete silence. She took a deep breath and glanced from side to side one last time before trying the door. Finding it unlocked, she pushed it open and stepped inside. Just as expected, the house was bare of all furniture or signs anyone lived here.

"Is anyone here?" She stayed close to the door, listening for any sign she wasn't alone.

"Hello? Bella?" A bark sounded from the direction of where she expected the kitchen to be. *Thank God, she's here.*

Bella continued barking, and it was enough for Lissa to gather her courage and move forward. She switched the duffle bag to her left shoulder and unstrapped the gun, wanting it accessible but out of sight. One step at a time, she edged through the living room, not wanting any surprises. It was the hardest thing ever not to run to Bella, but she had to be smart about this.

Bella's barking made it difficult to hear. Lissa tried to block out the familiar sound and strained to hear anything or anyone else moving around.

It was a swinging kitchen door, and Lissa placed one hand on it to push it open slowly. Inch by inch, she peered into the room as the crack opened her line of sight. *Bella.* Her baby was tied to a leash and hooked to the table.

Her heart exploded with joy, and all sense of caution disappeared. She darted to the table and scooped up Bella, snuggling her close. Several doggy licks later, Lissa pushed aside the overwhelming relief, knowing they were still in danger. They needed to get out of there. Fast. She set Bella down on the chair, tossed the duffel bag on the table, and bent to untie the leash.

Bella growled at the same time Lissa heard the sound behind her. Her hand went for the gun as she stood and spun around, coming face-to-face with a a tall, masked man, his gun pointed straight at her.

"Don't try anything stupid. Put your hands up. Any sudden moves, and you both die." The words came out muffled through the ski mask covering his entire head except for his eyes. Dark, menacing eyes. She put her hands in the air, terrified to do anything else. "What do you want?" Too late, she realized it also allowed her sweatshirt to ride up and reveal her weapon.

His gaze lowered, zeroing in on the gun. The man reached forward. Instinctively, Lissa took a step back.

"Not you, if that's what you're worried about. This is about money. Money, I deserve." He pulled her gun from her holster and stepped back. "It doesn't surprise me you carry, but I was prepared either way. I've been waiting a long time for this, every little detail planned. All I needed was the opportunity, and you took care of that nicely with the groomer appointment. I should thank you for making this easy."

"But how did you know about the appointment...unless...you tapped my phone lines." Lissa felt violated knowing the creep had been listening to everything. The thought had never crossed her mind, but then she hadn't known she was being targeted. "Why do you sound familiar? Who are you?" If possible, his eyes darkened further. They scrunched tighter.

"It doesn't matter. What matters, is that you sit down. And then we wait."

"Wait for what?" His voice was familiar, and Lissa tried hard to place it but kept drawing a blank. A tattoo was partially visible beneath the sleeve of his

T-shirt. It looked like the bottom half of a snake. Again, vaguely familiar, but she remained clueless as to the man's identity.

"I said sit," he snarled.

Lissa picked up Bella and held her tight to her chest for comfort as she sat down. If only she knew who this was, then maybe she could reason with the madman.

The man pulled a coil of rope from behind his back and moved to stand behind her. He wrapped the rope around her chest and arms and the back of the chair several times, securing it firmly in place. He tied a second rope around her legs. Bella continued to bark and growl, making Lissa afraid the man would grow short on patience and simply kill her.

"*Shhh*. Easy, Bella. It'll be okay." Lissa tried to soothe her with words, hoping against hope, Bella wouldn't snap at the man.

The guy went out of his way to keep his hands far from the vicinity of the dog's mouth.

"Now can you tell me what we're waiting for?" Bev would get her first text in a few minutes, and if Lissa didn't call her back before the appointed time, there was a good chance an army of police officers would start raining down on this address. She hated to think about what might happen to her and Bella if that happened and the madman was still here.

"You get to wait." He laughed, the sound not a nice one. "I have a note to deliver to your parents. I'd say your safe return is worth at least a cool million. I'm sure they consider your life is worth as much as Bella was to you."

The man pulled the duffel bag across the table, unzipped it, and peered inside. "What's this? You trying to screw me over?" The man slammed his hand down on the table, causing her to jump. Bella growled, hunching down in Lissa's lap with her teeth bared.

"You only gave me a day. No bank could give me that kind of money on short notice. Believe me, I tried. This is all the funds they would release until Monday. They started asking all sorts of questions about why I needed the money." Lissa was desperate to make him understand. She didn't want this bad situation to get worse.

"Monday, huh? Three days. Fine. I guess that means you're stuck here with me longer than you planned. And to make up for your shortage, the amount they need to give me just doubled to two million. I'll give them four days since there's a Sunday in there. See, I can be nice." His merciless laugh grated on her nerves.

The man grabbed the duffel bag and turned to leave. "I'll be back soon. And as insurance to keep you from doing anything stupid, like trying to escape, I'll take Bella with me."

He took a step toward her. Bella bared her teeth again, a ferocious continuous growl that threatened hand removal if the guy came any closer. "Easy, Bella." She tried to calm her, fearful of what the man would do.

"Never mind. I have a better idea." He grabbed the back of her chair and dragged it toward the swinging door. He pulled her through, stopping at the hall closet, shoving her and Bella inside before closing the door.

Lissa heard the lock clicking into place. Even if she could untie the tight ropes, it would be impossible to get out of a locked closet without any tools.

The sound of the front door slamming was still a welcome relief. Knowing the madman was no longer in the house gave her a chance to take a deep breath and try to figure out what to do next.

Chapter Fourteen

♥

DAMIEN HAD SPENT MOST of yesterday trying to ferret out clues from the ransom note. It hadn't helped SDS receptionist was out sick, and he'd ended up spending half the time answering telephones and dealing with people who walked in. It was a great relief when Marie walk through the front door this morning.

"Am I ever glad to see you. I think you deserve a raise. That phone rings off the hook, and I have no idea how you get things done."

Marie laughed. "It all works out. But if the boss man wants to give me a raise, who am I to complain?" She moved behind her desk to put away her purse and headed for the coffee machine.

"Did you hear the dog I was guarding got kidnapped?" He watched Marie closely. He didn't want to believe anyone in the office was involved, but he couldn't close his mind to the possibility. "Doesn't look good to have it happen on my watch."

"It's all over the papers. Ms. Walker hasn't been quiet about the fact she seems to think you're involved. You want a refill?" She held out the pot of coffee he'd made when he arrived earlier.

"Sure." He held out his cup. "It's already in the papers?"

"Oh yeah. Splashed across the front page yesterday. I'm surprised you didn't see it."

"I didn't look. I'm trying to figure out what's going on. I don't have much patience for the lies the media will spin to make a story. But it does explain why the phone was ringing off the hook yesterday."

"That woman doesn't know you very well, does she?" Marie sat in her chair and spun to face him.

"Well, no. But in all fairness, it doesn't look good when a ransom note comes in with SDS letterhead."

"I wondered about that myself when I read about it. I mean, how would someone get our letterhead?"

"That's the big question everyone wants answered. A detective was here yesterday grilling me with questions. Don't be surprised if he doesn't end up talking to everyone connected with SDS."

"I'll let the others know it's a possibility. We do get a little bit of foot traffic in here."

"But you would notice if a guy just walked in and tried to help himself to our letterhead paper. And I know you eat lunches at your desk. Have you noticed anyone acting weird when they were in here?"

Marie shook her head." I've been fighting the flu, and it kind of took over me. Everything from the last few days is a blur. I'm sorry."

"Well, if you think of anything, let me know. I'll take this back to my office and see what I can figure out. We are running out of time based on the dognapper's demands. They said three today, although I doubt they will hurt the dog. That would end their chances of getting anything, and these guys aren't usually going to go this far without getting something out of the deal." Frustrated at every turn, he could only hope Bella would remain safe.

"What's Miss Walker planning on doing?"

"Since she called the police and cast the investigation in our direction, I'm assuming she's letting them handle it. She hasn't spoken to me, so I don't really know what's happening on her end. Can't say as I blame her."

Damien gathered up his papers and thrust them in the file and turned to head down the hall.

"Wait a minute. I do remember something." Damien stopped and turned back.

"It was more like five days ago. There was a guy that came in asking me about hiring an investigator to check on his cheating wife."

"What makes him stand out in your mind?" He moved closer, excited about any possible lead that came his way.

"I remember he wasn't wearing a wedding ring. Which might be odd for a guy that's concerned about his wife."

"Good point. You have always been observant. One of the reasons you're fantastic at this job. Did you ever leave him alone in the office?"

"*Ummm*...yes. I'm sorry. I know that's against policy, but I suddenly started sneezing, and my nose was running, so I ran to the bathroom to blow my nose. I wasn't gone long, I swear."

"Don't worry. I trust you wouldn't have left the front office without good cause. But more importantly, it gives us our first promising lead. We've never had much use for the cameras we installed in here for security, but we do now. I'll be in my office reviewing the tape from that day. Let me know if you think of anything else."

"I'm sorry, Damien." Marie wasn't the reason Bella was stolen and letting her worry about any accidental part she may have played wouldn't be fair.

"Don't worry about it. I'm just glad you're feeling better. Now let's hope we can figure this out." He headed for his office, eager to cue up the video.

Using 4x speed, he watched the screen intently, hoping to find the cheating-wife guy. He paused, standing to stretch his back and refill his coffee. Not long after he settled back into the task of viewing the video, he spotted the man coming through the front door."

Adrenaline caused his heart to pound faster. He slowed the tape down to half the normal speed, not wanting to miss anything. Marie heading for the bath- room. The man moved across the office, nervously watching the hall where Marie had disappeared. The man grabbed what appeared to be a handful of letterhead paper from the print tray and slid them in his briefcase. He then moved to sit down in a chair on the other side of the room while he waited for Marie.

Absolute proof an employee wasn't responsible for the ransom note or the kidnapping. And evidence of who did. "Marie!" Do you have the file on that man? What's his name?"

"We never got that far. He was reluctant to give me any information. Did you find something?" Marie appeared at his door, a hopeful look on her face.

"Absolutely. It's our man. We need to figure out who he is and how to stop him before he gets away or hurts somebody." Damien took a few screenshots of the man. He had to get Lissa and see if she recognized him. It was time to put their differences aside to solve the case. "I'm going to see Miss Walker. See if you can Captain Miller to run this through the face- recognition system and get a name for me. And tell him what's going on, to be on the safe side."

"I'm on it." She leaned over to click a few buttons to send the image to her computer.

He grabbed the file and raced out the door, the knot in his stomach growing. He wouldn't be happy until he saw Lissa. Hopefully, she could solve the puzzle of the man's identity, and the police could pick him up before anything happened to Bella. He'd grown to love the little dog and had been worried about her ever since she'd been taken. Even though it was Lissa who'd left Bella with the groomer, it didn't matter. Damien felt equally guilty for not being there for her when she needed him most. She'd accused him of not doing his job, and it was unsettling to realize she was right. No wonder she hated him.

Damien pulled into the driveway and jumped out of the Jeep. He knocked on the front door, but there was no answer. Pulling out his key, he didn't hesitate to use it and enter her home. "Lissa!" He ran down the hall to the living room. "Anyone home?"

Only silence greeted him. He checked the garage and discovered her car missing. Where was she? He hoped the police weren't using her as bait at the ransom drop off to capture the guy. It wasn't unheard of, but surely they wouldn't resort to those tactics this early in the game. Johnny would have told him, or least he was almost positive his friend would. *Unless Lissa volunteered. Or unless she went alone.* Fear gripped him. She was headstrong enough to do precisely that.

He pulled out his phone and dialed the one person he knew she trusted explicitly and that might tell him what's going on. "Bev, it's Damien. Do you know where Lissa is? I'm at her place, and she's not here."

"What's wrong?" Bev wasn't cutting him any slack.

"Please, just tell me if you know where she's at. She may be in trouble. I may know who's behind the ransom note and the dognappings. I need to show her his mug shot to see if she can identify him." Damien ran a hand through his hair, frustrated Bev was choosing now to hold out on him.

"I don't know. She's pretty mad at you. But..." He could hear the worry in her voice as well.

"What is it?" he prompted.

"She did say something about meeting the ransom demands. I swear I thought I talked her out of it. But about five minutes ago, I got a text from her. It said if I hadn't heard from her by three forty-five to call the police and send them to the ransom address. I don't even know where that is." Bev's voice broke, worry laced in every word.

"It's 3:20 now, but I'm not waiting around to see if we hear from her. I know where she's at, and I'm going after her." Damien was already out the door.

"Keep me posted. And Damien, thanks. She can be a little hardheaded at times, and I fear she may have gone too far this time."

"Let's just hope you're wrong."

He put the Jeep in drive and punched the accelerator, the tires squealing as he raced down the driveway.

Chapter Fifteen

♥

IT WASN'T LONG BEFORE Surely the man hadn't come back already. She strained to listen as she rubbed Bella behind the ears, hoping to keep her quiet.

"Lissa," a voice called out. *Damien.* His presence confirmed what she'd suspected but hadn't wanted to accept. Damien was involved. *Why else would he be here?*

"Lissa?" he called out again. Bella barked, giving away her location. The dog always did have a soft spot for him, though usually, she was a better judge of character.

The closet door flew open, and light flooded the small room. Bella yipped with excitement, betraying Lissa with her turncoat excitement to see Damien.

"Thank God, you're all right! What were you thinking coming here alone? Were you out of your mind?"

Her eyes adjusted to the light change, her gaze zeroing in on Damien. "And who do you think was supposed to help me? The police weren't doing their job, and you can't be trusted. I came with my own protection, and I have a backup in place."

"You distrust me so much that you'd put yourself in danger?" Damien lifted his pant leg to reveal a knife strapped to his calf. He pulled the long blade from its sheath and came at her.

Stunned, she shook her head. "Please don't kill me. I'll get the money, I promise."

"Kill you? How many five and dime novels have you been reading in your spare time? I'm here to rescue you." Damien made short work of the ropes that bound her, finishing with a quick slice to the rope around her feet.

Lissa jumped to her feet, clutching Bella to her chest, unsure of what to believe. She was afraid to be wrong. Maybe it was the Little League coaching, or maybe it was their history, or maybe it was even the kiss, but she made a split-second decision to trust Damien. "The man's going to be back soon. He trapped me to blackmail my parents."

"Then let's get out of here." He grabbed her free hand and pulled her toward the door, peering out before continuing outside. "Coast is clear. Let's go."

The squeal of tires coming around the corner down the street caught their attention. A black car raced toward them.

Damien pushed her in the direction of his Jeep. "Get in the truck!"

Lissa headed for the Porsche instead. "My car. I'll drive." They didn't have time to argue, and she was relieved to see Damien follow her lead. She jumped in and handed him Bella. Lissa started the engine, threw it into drive, and raced away from the curb just as the black car was skidding to a halt behind her. She glanced in the rearview mirror to see the man jump out of the car and point a gun at them. Expecting a bullet at any second, she accelerated and swerved. No sound came. She glanced in the rearview mirror again and discovered the man hot on her tail.

"He's got a gun, and he's following us. I'm going to try to lose him." She focused on the road ahead, looking for the perfect spot to execute a quick turn.

"I've got a better idea. Let's get this guy off the street. I don't know who he is, but he needs to be behind bars once and for all." The anger in his voice surprised Lissa. Damien had always been an even- tempered guy, but this situation seems to have pushed all the wrong buttons.

Lissa made a sharp right turn, the car easily handling the maneuver. She needed to head for the outskirts of town and hoped to steer clear of anyone else getting hurt in the process. "What's your plan because this guy's not going anywhere."

"Do you know where the overpass is at Chapel Road off Highway 74?" Damien pulled out his phone and started to dial.

"Yes. You want me to head there?"

"Yes. I estimate we're about ten minutes away. Do you think you can keep him on your tail that long?"

"Please. You're asking me that question?" Lissa let out a laugh at the irony.

"Then do it. I'm calling for reinforcements." She couldn't help but admire his control and grasp of the situation.

"This is Damien Trent with SDS. Get Captain Miller on the phone. Stat. It's an emergency." Seconds seemed like minutes before he spoke again.

"Johnny? Listen, the dognapper case just turned into a kidnapping case. The guy is trying to blackmail Lissa Walker's parents. She was being held at 26 Maple Street, the drop-off location on the ransom note. I found her, and we got away, but he's hot on our tail. Can you get every available officer within a five-mile radius to the overpass at Chapel Road and Highway 74? We're going to lead the guy your way and let you take over, so he can't make a run for it and escape. He's driving what looks like a black Monte Carlo."

More silence.

"Thanks." Damien ended the call.

Lissa let out a sigh of relief. Help was on the way. "Close personal friend of yours I'm guessing? Not many people can command that kind of response."

"You could say that. Captain Miller is Johnny Miller. You know, the guy who went to school with us and played your boyfriend in the school play."

"I do remember." Lissa ran the stoplight and took a hard left turn, the wheels of the car slipping a little.

"Take that next left, there's a lot less traffic on that road."

"Gotcha. Don't look so worried, I could handle this with my eyes closed."

"Please don't." The sarcasm in his voice made her chuckle.

"It's just an expression. No eye closing, I promise. Relax. We got this."

Bella picked that moment to reach up and lick his face. "*Ugh.* Dog germs."

"You'll live." She chuckled and glanced in the rearview mirror again to make sure she didn't lose the creep.

"Do you know anything about the guy? I've got video footage of him and was bringing it to your place for you to look at and see if you recognized him."

"I wondered how you managed to show up to rescue me. Thanks, by the way. After everything I said, you probably hate me, and rightly so. As to the guy, he's familiar, but I can't figure it out. He had a hat on, and his face was covered, but there was a tattoo, and I swear I've seen it before." Lissa would find a way to make it up Damien when this was over. She'd wronged him and probably jeopardized his job with SDS.

"Well, if this plays out right, you'll get some answers. If you weren't driving ninety miles an hour, I'd show you the pictures. We're not far now." Damien spun around in his seat to check on their pursuer. "I'm not exactly sure what the police have worked out, so be ready to roll with whatever we see.

It might be best if we slow down as we approach, but don't make it too obvious."

"Yes, Mr. Trent, I'll slow down. No, Mr. Trent, I won't make it obvious. Are you always this bossy?" She laughed. They were both in control, but instead of being a competition, they were working together as a real team. It was a novelty for Lissa, and one she rather enjoyed.

"When it counts."

Lissa glanced over at him for a split second, but it was long enough to see him grin. Yes, they definitely needed to talk when this was over. It was high time she told him the truth about how she felt.

Damien's phone rang. "What's up? We are about a minute or two out. Let me put you on speakerphone."

"Instead of going under the pass, we want you to come up the exit ramp. There's nowhere to go from there, and we've got it blocked at the top and will close off the bottom the second he exits. We've got one car space available for you to squeeze through the middle of our roadblock, and we'll close it the second you go through.

Think you can handle that, Lissa?" Johnny was in his element, the excitement of the chase unmistakable in his voice.

"You know it, Johnny, Let's do this." Lissa couldn't deny her own rush of adrenaline. She wanted to stop this creep, and it felt good to be a part of the plan to put this guy behind bars.

"Atta girl."

She came to the ramp and exited, the sharp curve blocking her vision at the top. Just as predicted, the black car followed her. She accelerated, giving herself more time to squeeze through the opening they'd left. After she cleared the roadblock, she slid the car to a stop. She wanted the satisfaction of facing off with the guy who had dared to steal Bella and threaten her and her parents.

"I'm not sure they had it in mind for you to be a part of the showdown." Damien grabbed her arm to stop her from getting out of the car.

"There's no way I'm missing it."

"Stubborn woman." He let her go, and she slid out of the car. Seconds later, she heard the car door slam behind her. Damien caught up to her. She glanced up at him, comforted by his presence.

The whole thing was over in seconds. The man was surrounded by police. Guns drawn; he didn't stand a chance. He got out of the car, hands in the air.

He reached for her arm. "Hold up. This is close enough. They've got him, and we need to let the police do their job without anyone getting hurt or any mistakes."

"Yes, Mr. Trent." She grinned up at him.

"I like the sound of that." Wise guy. There would never be a dull moment between them if she could convince him to give them a chance.

"Hey, Johnny." Damien reached out to shake hands with his friend. "Hey, you two. Nice driving, Lissa. We need to talk later about what you were doing at that house in the first place, but I'll get your statement later. Dang crazy thing to do, if you ask me."

"And me," Damien chimed in.

"So, what's his story?" Lissa wasn't close enough to see who it was yet.

"Claims he's innocent, but there's a black bag with two-hundred-thousand dollars in it that leads me to believe he's not as innocent as he says. You know anything about that?"

"Sort of." Lissa smiled. "That would be mine." Johnny shook his head, not at all surprised.

"It was the ransom money."

"I figured as much. The guy doesn't have any ID on him. We're running his tags now." Johnny added a few notes to his little black book.

"Can I get closer to get a look at him? There's something familiar about him."

"Sure." He shrugged. "Could make things easy for us."

She followed Johnny, Damien still by her side. The man was being held in handcuffs and pressed up against the police cruiser.

"Spin him around, Dan, and let's get a good look at him. Pull off his hat and bandana." Officer Dan made short work of complying.

It couldn't be. "Jasper?" This didn't make any sense. *Why would he do this to her?* She knew the answer even as she asked herself the question. *Her parents.*

"I take it you know him," Johnny asked.

"His name is Jasper London. We dated in college. Turned out to be a real jerk and more interested in my parents than me. And apparently, he still is." She wrapped her arms around her midsection, trying to stop the pain of the past from surfacing. Why now, after all these years?

"You ruined my life," Jasper shouted at her. "It's all your fault. Everything."

"I don't know what you're talking about." We broke up. Not a big deal. Not enough for you to do this." She needed answers, needed to understand.

"I needed money, and you ruined it all. I've spent the last five years trying to recover from almost being killed because I couldn't repay a gambling debt. Your parents wouldn't have noticed until it was too late if I pirated their newest release that year. It would have been a drop in the bucket compared to the millions and millions they made. No one would have gotten hurt. Five years, I've spent digging my way out of that. And since it all started with you, I thought it should all end with you. You and your stupid dog."

"That stupid dog was smart enough to know you were a jerk, something I had to figure out for myself." She couldn't believe she'd ever dated a guy like him, and it left her wondering about her judgment in people in general. She never seemed to get it right.

"Get in the car, mister. It's over." The officer pushed down on Jasper's shoulder to assist him into the back of the cruiser.

A white van with a satellite dish on top pulled up. The local news station was quick to follow the police scanner and was never far behind the action. The story would be all over the six o'clock news tonight. The cameraman was out of the van and filming within seconds.

"I've got to go back to the station to file reports. Make sure I can reach you to get your statements. I'd love to catch up some time. It's been great to see you two back together. I didn't think you two had ever made it work."

"We didn't." They answered in unison, but the crisp tone of Damien's voice told her something was bothering him.

"Shame." Johnny shook his head and waved as he left.

Damien reached out to pet the scruff of Bella's neck. "Lissa, I'm glad you're okay. I think you're crazy, but I'm glad it worked out all right. It took a lot of guts to do what you did. I guess that's what you do when you love something enough to put everything else aside."

"Thanks. I hope you'll—"

"Miss Walker? Sam Holder, Channel 8 News. We'd love to get a story about what just happened. We understand this is the guy who stole all the other dogs you rescued, and that you helped take him down in a high-speed chase."

The man shoved a camera in her face, and Lissa went into an automatic-response mode, knowing what she needed to do. As much as she'd rather get in her car and go home to have a much-needed conversation with Damien, she knew this was part of the routine, and it was expected of her. She shot Damien an apologetic shrug before turning on her megawatt smile and transforming into media mode.

"We worked together with law enforcement, that is correct."

"I heard it was some pretty fancy driving. Was that you?" The man was fact checking, and she couldn't fault him for wanting to get the story right.

"Also correct information." She laughed. "I have it on good authority, I was up to the task." Everyone joined in to laugh with her.

"Your bodyguard was with you? Does this mean he's off the hook as a suspect?" It was sure to be the question uppermost in everyone's mind after the very public dressing down she'd given Damien.

"He wasn't my bodyguard. He was Bella's guard. And now that the dognapper has been arrested, his services are no longer required. And, no, he's no longer under suspicion. In fact, SDS has been cleared of any and all involvement. The letterhead paper from the ransom note was stolen from the company's office to frame them, and I regret any accusations I made otherwise." It was important she repair any damage she could while she had the media's full attention.

"I'm sure that's been a huge relief for Damien Trent. The reputation of his company will be fully restored with this recent development in the case." The man smiled and nodded.

"What do you mean *his* company?" She didn't like the implication of the man's comment at all, because if it were true, what she'd done was ten times worse.

"Damien Trent owns SDS. Are you saying you didn't know that?" Lissa took several deep breaths, this new bit of information hard to grasp and totally unexpected.

"No comment." Lissa shook her head and turned, scanning the people milling about in search of Damien.

He was nowhere to be found.

Lissa didn't doubt for an instant the man had his facts straight. She'd made a royal mess of everything, and all because she'd been afraid to trust Damien. As soon as she got back to the house, she intended to clear the air and apologize.

If he lets me. She'd accused him of stealing Bella and then proceeded to trash his company's reputation. What reason did he have to give her another chance?

After stopping at the station to give her statement, she was exhausted and ready to go home. She still couldn't believe the fake groomer was Jasper's girlfriend.

It hadn't taken the police long to pick her up and bring her in, booking her on charges of impersonation, dognapping, and accessory to kidnapping and blackmail. The woman had been more than willing to talk in the hope she'd get a plea-bargain deal.

He'd promised her marriage and an easy life if she stopped by the groomers, picked up a business card, and then showed up at Lissa's to grab Bella. He promised her it would be easy, and that nothing could go wrong. The poor woman had thought he loved her. Jasper didn't know the meaning of the word.

Lissa pulled into her driveway. She cradled Bella in her arms as she entered the house and called out to Damien. His lack of response multiplied the gnawing that had begun growing in her stomach from the minute she'd learned he owned SDS.

She climbed the stairs and made her way to his room. Pushing open the door, she quickly figured out he'd taken all his clothes and left. It was more than enough proof to know it was over between them. Lissa shook her head and clung to Bella.

"I'm sorry, baby. I drove him away. I know you liked him. I liked him, too. A lot." Bella rubbed her bristly face up against Lissa's cheek, mixed in with little doggy kisses.

"I really messed up, girl." She let out a heavy sigh and turned away to head back downstairs. She poured a glass of wine and sat down in the living room, with Bella curled up against her leg. Lissa stroked the dog's back, using her favorite scratch technique. It was great to have her baby home, and for that she was grateful.

But Damien's absence left a new hole in her heart. Damien had never been after her money or publicity. Everything he'd done had either been for her because he cared, or because it was his job. And it was up to her to find out which. She owed him that much.

In high school, she'd let him go without a fight and hadn't bothered to figure out what went wrong. She wouldn't make the same mistake twice. There were so many what-ifs, but none greater than the what if of not going after him this time. There had to be some way to compromise between his need for privacy and her need for publicity. It's not like all the hoopla was for her personally, not even close. Even the proceeds from her signature fragrance were to help shelters all across the country. Didn't that count for something?

The phone rang, jarring the silence of the empty house.

"Hey, Bev," she said, seeing her friend's name splashed across the screen. She'd forgotten about the scheduled text.

"Is everything okay? I had to hear what was going on from the news. The police wouldn't even tell me anything even though I'm the one who called them just like you said to do. Why haven't you called? And Damien promised to keep me informed. I was worried sick."

"I'm sorry. I forgot you knew with everything else happening. Bella and I are home. Everything's fine. Or almost fine." She fought back the tears threatening to spill over. This afternoon had taken its toll on her emotions, and she was a wreck.

"What do you mean?" Bev deserved the truth. The whole truth.

"I found out Damien owns SDS. He was never involved and was only trying to help me. I made such horrible and very public accusations. I'm such a terrible person, and he hates me. He's gone."

"Stop. You were upset, and the evidence pointed in his direction. What else could you have possibly thought?"

"I never told you what really happened." Lissa relayed what she'd heard that night at the party.

If not for her crazy emotions, she might have handled it differently. Which made her wonder just how much of her over-the-top response had been because of the note and how much because of the attention Damien was doling out to the women. There was still the issue of him not standing up for her, but she owed it to him to ask, not assume. At no point, and especially in light of the kiss, had he ever made her think he would laugh at her behind her back.

"Wow. You like this guy. A lot." Her friend zeroed in on the heart of the matter much quicker than Lissa. It had taken her years to realize that what was in her heart wasn't going away, no matter how hard she tried.

"It would seem so. But my history with men doesn't do much for my confidence. And don't forget, Damien *was* one of those guys." Except he wasn't the same guy. Mostly, he was. But stronger, more determined.

"What are you going to do about it?"

"I don't know. What should I do?" She would take any advice at this point.

"You said he was really into racing before. I could send over some pit passes. Maybe if you could entice him to the track, it would give you two a chance to talk."

"Great idea. Can you send the passes over with a note of apology? Coming from you, he's less likely to toss it in the trash without even opening the envelope."

"I'm on it. And good luck. I think you need to show him how you feel. Take a chance on love."

Love.

Defining the emotion made it real. Tangible. Maybe the answer all along wasn't about joining two different worlds, but about exchanging one world for something different. Love was putting someone else's needs above her own. Just like she'd done with Bella. Damien deserved so much more, and she had the power to give it. "Can I ask you something?"

"Sure."

"Do you think I'd make a good spokesperson and manager for the new rescue shelter?"

"Absolutely. But it would be a full-time job to do it justice. Not something you really have time to fit in your busy schedule. Why?"

"I'm just thinking over some things." She didn't want to say anything yet, because she hadn't thought it through. This was her decision to make, and it was a big one. It wouldn't be fair to lay it at the feet of her best friend. "Like?"

"Just things. Let me know if you hear that Damien is going."

"Meaning you're not going to tell me. Have it your way. You'll tell me when you're ready. Oh, and don't forget Prince Dorian will be at the race Sunday. He's bringing Gatsby. Bella will be so excited."

"Yes, for sure. I was thrilled when he emailed to say he was coming. Of course, I'll stop by and see him before the race, assuming I make it in the qualifying round to get to the big race on Sunday."

"You'll be fine. I have complete faith in your abilities, and with Bella back, your focus will be exactly where it needs to be. The other drivers are in for another rude awakening thanks to you."

"As my marketing manager, you have to say that." Lissa laughed.

"But as your friend, I'm just telling you like it is."

Chapter Sixteen

♥

As it turned out, Bev was right. Lissa placed seventh in the pole qualifier, earning her an excellent position for the race today. Even Razor's surly attitude didn't take away from the thrill of finishing with one of the top qualifying times. Of course, it made things even better when Bev told her Damien had accepted the pit passes. It sounded like he might actually attend.

Lissa arrived at the track early to meet with her crew. She made it a personal rule to cover her check- list one last time before the start of the race, even after the stock cars passed the morning inspection. She trusted her team, but she trusted her own instincts more. As the driver, it gave her a level of comfort. Traveling at speeds over two-hundred miles per hour left no room for mistakes with her abilities or the car.

Bev stood nearby holding Bella, the two of them cute together with their earmuffs firmly in place. It was a matter of necessity to protect their hearing from the thunderous roar of the engines this close to the action.

"Looks good, Mack." Her crew chief stayed on top of the guys, and therefore on top of the action. The crew tested every spare tire, stacking them in preparation for any pit stops. The Walker Racing mechanic's booth was set up, and everything was ready for fast access. Her pit crew had worked tirelessly to perfect their teamwork over the past years, cutting the pitstop time considerably. Getting back into the lineup after the yellow caution flag was lifted was critical to positioning and winning races.

"What did you find out about that fluid leak from the brake line?" Lissa leaned over to check the hose attachments in the engine.

"One of the seals needed replacing, but it's all good now." Mack nodded reassuringly.

"Perfect."

"It's going to be hot today, and the tracks are going to heat up fast. It will be tough on the tires, so we need to plan for the possibility. Focus on engine braking right before the turns and maybe we can save at least one change out."

"I hear you. It's the longest race on the circuit, and the weather is unseasonably hot. A lot will depend on how the other teams handle this."

"That's true." Mack waved at one of the crew members. "I need to talk to Jeff. See you in a bit."

"Gotcha." Lissa searched for Bev. She wasn't prepared for the sight of Damien standing next to her friend, the two of them deep in conversation. He looked good. Dressed in jeans, boots, and a T-shirt with *Walker Racing* splashed across the front, more than likely courtesy of Bev, the man was droolworthy. Or maybe it had been a few days too long since she'd last seen him. Whatever it was, it took everything she had not to rush to his side, apologize, throw herself into his arms, and beg for another chance.

Damien glanced her way as she approached, but his expression remained unreadable.

"Hey there. I'm glad you could make it." Lissa smiled, hoping to ease the awkwardness.

"Thanks for the invite and the ticket. It's been a long time since I've been to a race." Still non-committal, but it was a start. At least they were talking.

Bev looked back and forth between her and Damien, the gleam in her eyes all too telling. Lissa hoped she hadn't been talking out of turn with Damien, trying to advance Lissa in his good graces. It was up to her to fix the damage she'd done. If it were possible.

"I'm counting on you to be my good-luck charm."

"I doubt you need that. You had a great qualifying time."

Enough of the small talk. It was time to be brave and own up to her mistake. She took a deep breath. "Thanks. Listen, I wanted to—"

"Lissa, it's great to see you." Prince Dorian joined them, cutting off her apology to Damien with a hug. Dressed in a Gucci suit and loafers, the prince didn't look like your typical race fan—but that's where the differences ended between him and every other race fanatic that had come to witness the action today. Whenever Dorian was in the country, he made it a point to attend the races and look her up.

"Prince Dorian, it's so good to see you." Lissa reached up to scratch Gatsby behind the ears. "Hey, boy, how are you?" Dorian's corgi was never far away, the guy as crazy about him as she was about Bella. It was one of the things that had drawn them together in the first place. Since then, they'd become good friends.

"Glad you're okay, little one." Dorian rubbed Bella's back as she tried to lick his hand.

"You know Bev, and this is Damien Trent, a friend of mine. Damien, this is Prince Dorian of Avington, and a dear friend of mine."

Dorian took Bev's hand and kissed the back of it and then turned to Damien. "It's a pleasure to meet you. I've not seen you here before." Lissa wasn't sure what to make of the way the two men sized each other up.

"Good to meet you also." They shook hands.

"Actually, it's my first time here in nine years."

"So not a die-hard fan, I take it?" Dorian laughed, shaking his head as if he couldn't imagine anyone not being one.

"I was once upon a time, but someone changed that for me. It does feel good to be back." Damien glanced at her as he emphasized the word "someone," the implication all too obvious.

Lissa frowned at Damien. He couldn't possibly blame her for his decision to stop following racing.

The prince turned to Lissa. "I was worried about you and Bella when I heard the news. I was just about to send some of my security team to help you try to find her. You should have said something to me sooner."

"That's sweet of you. We're doing great, all things considered. It was awful, but now my focus is back where it needs to be, just in time for today's race."

"That's good. You're the face of tomorrow night's charity event, and we can't have you in tears. Although, maybe it would bring in more money for the shelter." He laughed.

"Hey, can we get a picture of the two of you together?" A cameraman approached them even as Prince Dorian's bodyguards stepped forward to stop the man.

"That's fine with me if you're okay with it." Dorian thought it was her face that helped the rescue center cause, but it certainly didn't hurt that he was a firm advocate and leading contributor.

Dorian shrugged. She knew he wasn't a fan of the media. It was another thing they had in common. People didn't understand that no matter how famous celebrities were, they were still human beings who needed privacy at times.

She reached for Bella. "Let's do this with our little sweethearts. They love the limelight."

The prince put his other arm around her and smiled. He loved Gatsby and didn't mind showing him off.

Damien stood off to the side, a scowl on his face.

Lissa kept smiling for the pictures as the camera clicked away, shot after shot. After the photographer left, she relaxed.

"Glad that's over. I only agreed because it was you." Dorian dropped his arm and stepped away.

"They can't do much harm with pics of us and our dogs. You'll survive." She laughed. "Besides, it gives them something to talk about."

"Let's hope not." Dorian shook his head and dropped a kiss on her cheek. "Good luck out there today. I saw you at the qualifying round. Looking good as always."

"Thanks. You've always been one of my biggest fans."

"That's because you're different. And you don't kowtow to me when I come around. It gets tiring, trust me."

"You need better friends." She laughed.

Dorian said his farewells and left, his body-guard two steps behind him.

"You two seem pretty close." Damien's words came out as a statement, not a question. If she didn't know any better, she'd think he was jealous, especially after witnessing his scowl earlier. It gave her hope.

"We're friends." She shrugged, enjoying the twist this conversation had taken just a little too much.

"Is that so?"

"Yes, that's so. Listen, before he arrived, I was trying to apologize for not trusting you. I said some awful things, and I hope you can forgive me. Chalk it up to stress and my past. I know it doesn't justify what I did, but I do hope you can find a way to give me another chance. As friends, of course." She blushed, her words making it sound like they were a couple or something.

"Don't worry about it. You've got bigger things on your mind right now. Take care out there and be safe."

It wasn't the answer she'd hoped for. Not by a long shot. "I've got to go. See you after the race." She hugged Bella, gave her a kiss, and handed her back to Bev.

"Go get 'em, Maneater." Bev laughed. "Chew those guys up into little hunks of metal and spit their sorry butts back out."

Lissa shook her head and laughed as she walked away. She secured her helmet in place and took one last look back at Damien. Their gazes met and held for a moment before she turned away. It was time to shut out the rest of the world. It was just her, the crew, and the race.

The team all gathered around, said a prayer, and then cheered her on with moral support. Mack hugged her, giving her a pat of encouragement on the back.

Lissa slid in through the window of the car and strapped herself in. She flipped the switch to start the engine. After adjusting her headset and running a test with Mack, she gave him the thumbs up, ready to run a few warm-up laps. The crowd disappeared, as did the roar of the engines all around her. It was just her, the raw power of the vehicle, and the track. With one last glance at Damien, she pulled out on pit road, following the car in front of her as they all started the warm-up routine around the track. She steered from side to side, warming up the tires. A rush of adrenaline sent her heart beating in overtime. *It was time.*

Damien wanted to accept Lissa's apology, but her lack of trust had stung. He'd been surprised when Bev called him about the pit pass, and the race fan in him hadn't been able to say no. And if he was honest, the idea of seeing her again held an even greater appeal.

What he hadn't expected though, was Prince Dorian. The man's arm wrapped around her was a reminder of everything different between him and Lissa. Totally at ease, she'd chatted with the prince as if it were nothing special. He, on the other hand, was content to remain low key. Jeans versus a Gucci suit. Damien didn't stand a chance in Lissa's world. Neither of them seemed to mind the invasion of their privacy. Instead, they'd embraced it and smiled for the camera, whereas Damien despised it.

Lissa pulled out on the track, and Damien suddenly found it hard to breathe. It would be easy to blame it on the fumes, but more likely, it was watching Lissa and knowing the danger out on the track. It took sheer guts to get out there and race, but she clearly loved it. No one could have guessed the wallflower of Bellevue

High would be the one to claim the title of most successful in their graduating class.

Bev came to stand next to him, Bella still safely ensconced in her arms. "You okay? You seem a little tense."

"I've never been down in the pit. The sights and sounds are a little overwhelming the first time." He watched the track intently as Lissa lapped it yet again, bumper to bumper with the car in front of her. Damien held his breath as they reached the turn.

"Are you sure that's all?"

"What do you mean?" He stayed focused on the track, not wanting Bev to see the truth in his eyes.

"Nothing to do with Lissa, right? Here, why don't you take Bella for a minute? She's getting heavy." Bev held the dog out, forcing him to look at her.

"Sure. This isn't about Lissa." He pulled the dog in close against his chest as she nuzzled his neck with her cold nose.

"I'm good at reading people. I'm not sure you're being honest with me, but the question is are you at least being honest with yourself?" Thankfully, Bev turned away to watch the race, giving him a second to form an answer that might satisfy the woman.

"It wouldn't matter. She and I have a history that we can't seem to get past."

"I wouldn't be so sure. You've missed a lot in the last nine years, and I know her. Safe to say, better than you at this point."

Damien didn't want to hope, because it wouldn't change a thing, but he couldn't stop himself from wanting to know more. "I'm listening."

"Before I tell you what I know, answer me one question. Why did you really cut Lissa out in high school? I need to make sure my trust in you isn't misplaced." Bev's gaze was unwavering.

"I was young and stupid. Lissa changed almost overnight. Her parents' success went to her head, and I couldn't handle the new Lissa. She craved the attention, I hated it. I never stopped caring about her, I just watched from the distance because I didn't want to be a part of the world she'd entered. We were on two different paths." Maybe he was still being stupid by shutting her out. He didn't know what to believe anymore.

"I heard you called her a spoiled, rich kid? That doesn't seem like someone who still cared and watched from the sidelines." Bev's insistence caught him off-guard.

"I've never said that about her."

"Well, a friend of hers said you did. Imagine how she felt."

"Wow. Not cool."

"Exactly. And after you ditched her, the quarterback in high school used her to get to her parents.

Then there's the crazy lunatic who kidnapped Bella. He dated her in college only to get to her parents. And the other night, you laughed at Lissa with a group of women belittling her skills as a racer. She's had a lot of people make it hard for her to trust anyone."

"Wait a minute. What are you talking about? I didn't make fun of Lissa. I defended her in a way that stopped the conversation in its tracks and left the others laughing."

"That's not what she saw. And then the ransom note came. All I'm saying is you might want to reconsider shutting her out because she didn't trust you. She's had good reason not to trust anyone most of her life."

"I didn't know."

"What are you going to do about it? She deserves it."

"I don't know. I'll talk to her and see where we stand. I can't promise more than that."

The stock cars all lined up. The noise of the crowd was nothing compared to the roar of the engines. But Damien only had eyes for the number seventeen car. *Lissa.*

The light turned green, and they were off, Damien periodically reminding himself to breathe.

Bella seemed equally intent on the race as if sensing Lissa was out there.

Lap after lap, the cars raced by. An hour had passed before Bev showed up and handed him a sandwich and a water. "Here. You need to keep hydrated. It's a long race."

She fed Bella a few treats.

"Thanks."

"I've got a couple seats over here if you want to join me."

"Great."

"What's between her and that prince?"

"Dorian? Nothing. They're friends."

"Didn't look like it to me."

"It's all for the camera. The media loves Lissa, and she gives them what they want. And then she gets what she wants."

"And what is that?"

"To raise money for the rescue shelter." Damien felt like a fool. Lissa wasn't all about the money for herself, it was for the animals. Of course, she'd put herself out there for them, she had a heart the size of the Grand Canyon.

A loud crashing note combined with the sudden silence of the crowd alerted Damien and Bev there was trouble on the track. They jumped to their feet and rushed to the pylon barriers to see what was happening.

Damien watched as cars sped by, searching for Lissa each time she came around. The yellow caution light lit up the board. The cars slowed. The smoke cleared, and Damien couldn't breathe when he saw her car against the sidewall facing backward. Another car sat on the track sideways with a third mashed into its front end.

He hoped she was okay. Ambulances shot out of pit road and headed toward the accident scene. *Please Lord, let her be okay.*

Her car moved. It was a good sign. Lissa turned her car around and waved out the window to the crowd and to the rescue team to alert them she was okay. She pulled up behind the other cars now being held up as they cleared the wreckage.

Damien breathed a sigh of relief. At that moment, he knew the truth. He loved her. The thought of losing her forever made every inch of his body ache with fear. Public life. Private life. What did it matter as long as he could share it with her? He'd been a fool to walk away once before, and he had no intention of doing it again.

Chapter Seventeen

♥

LISSA TOOK A DEEP breath. In and out. Close calls and collisions always shook her up, but then she was positive it had the same effect on the guys. They were just too macho to admit it. She glanced at Bella's photo taped to the dash and said a prayer of thankfulness. She'd been lucky only to be caught on the side and spun around, but the adrenaline rush was the same as if it had been her in the tangled mess. She prayed the other drivers were uninjured.

There were always risks, something every driver knew when they got on the track. Over the years, several lives had been lost in the sport, but as daunting as it seemed at the time, passion for the sport kept the drivers coming back for more. Being a legend or a rookie didn't matter, any crash could wipe out a car or a driver.

She pulled into the pit, slowing to the posted speed. Mack and the rest of the crew jumped into action the second she stopped, checking over the car. They changed all four tires and topped off her fuel. Lissa watched as the current leader pulled back onto pit road, followed by several other drivers.

Come on, guys. She revved the engines, eager to be off. Every second pushed her further back in the lineup.

"Go. Go. Go," Mack yelled when they finished.

She pulled into the lineup, careful to watch her speed. The last thing she needed was a speeding ticket that would put her at the end of the lineup as everyone was repositioned to follow the lead car.

They all followed the pace car around the track, warming up their tires and brakes. After several laps, the light turned green, the pace car dipped into pit road. Positioning at this point was key. She hugged the outside wall and then tucked down in the curve, coming up ahead of the car in front of her. It was a good restart, and she needed to capitalize on it. "All clear."

"Three more ahead of you. After the next one, you have a stretch of five or six car lengths to make up some ground on the lead two." Mack was quick to keep her advised with advanced planning. Her timing had to be perfect if she wanted to win, and she did—for Damien and Bella.

The side-swipe collision might have shaken her up a bit, but it had also provided her with clarity regarding her life. All her had doubts faded away. And in their place was a confidence about the next steps to take. Steps that included Damien if she could convince him to give them a chance. They owed it to each other.

Lissa rounded the turn and passed the car ahead of her. She stomped on the gas pedal and the car jumped forward under the massive RPM burst as she hit the straightaway. Lap after lap, she pressed harder and harder, trying to close the lengths between her and the two lead cars. It was hot and grueling, but she was in her element. It was as though an angel was guiding her through the cars.

On and on they raced. Thirty-three laps later, Lissa saw her opening.

"Taking it tight on four. Going inside." She clued the crew into her intentions.

"Easy does it to keep from drifting high." Mack's warning fell on deaf ears. She was all in, and easy had no place on the track.

She slid by number thirty-seven and pulled into second place. "All clear."

"That was risky."

"Lighten up. It worked. We need to take chances. What's the lap count?" she asked.

"Twenty-two on next pass." Mack had been with her from the beginning of her racing career, and sometimes she wondered if he was a little more cautious because she was a woman. With some guys, it wasn't an insult, because it came from caring. Five hundred and seventy-eight laps into this race and she was still in it.

Darkness started to close in over the track, the bright lights casting a hazy glow over the area. Lissa pushed harder down the straight-away, bumping the tail of the lead car. *Get a move on or get out the way.*

"Easy. Don't make him mad." Mack came across the headset.

"I'm going to do a fake high-side rush. Let's see if this guy bites. If he does, he's going down."

"Eight laps at next pass. Go for it. Show him what you're made of. No sugar and spice running in the Maneater's veins." Mack laughed. "Open it up and trust your instincts."

"Roger that." Lissa braced herself as she let the car drift high. The leader moved to block her ever so slightly, just enough for her to make a move. She muscled the car left, dropping low as she gunned it, hoping they didn't connect as she passed.

Nothing happened. She let out the breath she'd been holding. "All clear."

"You got it! You got it! Finish strong and watch your backside." Mack's excitement rippled through the headset.

Lissa pushed harder, the finish line in sight. One last turn and she was home free. She flew past the black and white checkered line. She couldn't believe it. *She'd won.* The hometown crowd was on their feet cheering.

Her arms felt like spaghetti as she made her way around the track. The other cars pulled into the pit.

"Woohoo! Nice work, Lissa. You did it!" Mack and the guys stood close to the pit road wall and cheered as she passed

"I can't believe it." Lissa brushed away her tears. Being a woman in a man's world didn't mean she didn't get emotional.

She raced around the track, spun out in turn two, and stopped at turn one as the official came out to meet her.

"Congratulations, Lissa." The official handed her the American flag.

"Thanks, Stan." She sped away toward the finish line, flag flying, and blew a few donuts to honor the crowd. She took a few more laps around the track before heading into pit road to celebrate with her crew. And Damien.

Her gaze zeroed in on Damien. He stood smiling with Bella tucked under his arm. Bev stood next to him, waving her hands and jumping up and down. Lissa slid out the window and removed her helmet, waving to the crowd amidst the cheers.

The crew all took turns hugging her. It was a team win, and everyone there knew it.

She turned to Damien only to discover he'd handed Bella over to Bev. At that moment, every- thing else faded away as he held out his hand to her.

"Congratulations." He grinned, pulling her against his chest. He leaned down and captured her lips in a kiss before she could answer. The deafening roar of the crowd reached her ears.

She stepped back. "Wow. Nice congratulations kiss." She laughed. Winning the race was great, but kissing Damien was amazing, and there was no way she was letting him go without a fight. If she could win the Coca-Cola 600, she could win his heart.

Twenty minutes later, they made their way to the grandstand. The race officials made a short speech and then handed her the trophy while the crowd cheered. She'd come a full circle. Looking around, Lissa couldn't feel more honored than she did at this moment. These people cared. Her gaze drifted to Damien. The past and the present collided in that second.

Lissa took a deep breath and let it out slowly, making a decision she'd avoided for some time because she wasn't sure. Any hesitation disappeared. The answer was waiting for her at the bottom of the steps. *Damien.*

It was time for a new direction. "Thank you all for your love and support. You guys rock!" She held up the trophy, and the crowd stood and cheered. Lissa talked about the race and commented on the great efforts by the other drivers, making sure to give credit where credit was due. "Before I go, I have a few things I want to say. First, most of you probably know Bella, my corgi, was recently dognapped. She's back with me safe and sound—" Lissa pointed at her baby, "—because of the fantastic security efforts and dedication from SDS, as well as the cooperation of our local law enforcement. I just wanted to set the record straight, since once upon a time, I said otherwise." She grinned as the crowd cheered her on even more.

"My second announcement may come as a shock, but it's something I've considered for the past few months, and today's win makes it easy. I'm retiring from racing. Today was my last race. I can't think of a better way to finish since I started my professional winning career right here at the Charlotte Motor Speedway. Thank you all for your love and support over the years."

Lissa waved to the crowd, the deafening roar making it impossible to say anything else. She started down the steps, her focus on Damien. He stood there watching her, a stunned look of surprise on his face. It was good to know she could shake him up occasionally.

Fireworks exploded into the night, lighting up the sky in a burst of color.

"I hope you'll join me for the celebration party." There was a lot she wanted to tell him, but right now wasn't the time.

"We need to talk, but not now. This is your moment to shine, and I'd love to share it with you." Damien reached for her hand and pulled her close.

"And tomorrow night? The charity event starts at seven. Can I also expect you to attend with me?" Lissa knew he hated the public events, but she hoped he would consider coming. There had to be some give and take if this was going to work.

"Absolutely. Anywhere you go, I'm in." He dropped a kiss on her mouth.

Several of the drivers came over to congratulate her.

"I'll be right here. You're the star tonight" He stepped off to the side.

The guys joked around quite a bit, but they gave her total respect. She noticed Razor approaching and tensed when Damien stepped in front of him, halting the jerk's progress. Maybe it would always be this way, Damien to the rescue. Truth be told, she kind of liked it.

The two men exchanged words, and then surprisingly, Damien stepped aside.

Razor joined the group. "Good job out there. Congratulations." It was forced, but it was a huge step in the right direction.

"Thank you. It looks like you did pretty good out there today, too."

"I focused on fixing my inferior car." He grinned and walked away. Razor's comment set the guys off laughing. The story of the putdown she'd fired off at Razor had clearly made the rounds on the circuit. The others wandered off, leaving her alone with Damien.

"I heard you talking about your retirement with the guys. Out of curiosity, why are you retiring?" Damien asked.

"I'm ready for a change." Lissa led the way back to the pit.

"Meaning?"

"We'll talk about it. Later. Just like you said."

Bev caught up with her first. "Congratulations. Looks like you won more than a race." Her friend winked; a teasing smile plastered on her face.

"Maybe." Lissa grinned, shooting a glance at Damien couldn't hear them.

"There's no maybe in the way he watches you all the time. You should have seen him when you almost crashed into that wall. I thought he was going to go crazy. It was so sweet."

"You and I have different ideas of sweet." Lissa laughed.

"Don't look now, but the prince has arrived, probably to offer his congratulations. Talk about a Triple Crown winner. First, the race, then Damien, and now the prince."

"But only one of those really matters."

"The question is, which one?" Bev pressed her for an answer, one that even Lissa wasn't prepared to admit.

Luckily, Dorian's arrival ended the discussion.

Chapter Eighteen

♥

Damien pulled up to Lissa's house and got out, adjusting his tie and coat. The dark-blue suit usually stayed tucked away in the depths of his closet, but tonight, he was pulling out all the stops. After bringing an exhausted Lissa home last night, he'd kissed her goodnight and left, knowing today was soon enough to tell her how he felt.

He rang the doorbell and waited. Even though he had a key, it was more date like to knock.

Lissa opened the door to greet him, her smile reaching her eyes. She was dressed in a sleeveless yellow dress, the satiny material emphasizing every soft curve of her body. He was glad she didn't hide her athletic figure, because, without a doubt, she was one sexy woman.

"You look stunning." Damien leaned forward to kiss her.

"Thank you. You look pretty good yourself. I wasn't even sure you owned a suit." She laughed.

"I'm glad you approve. Contrary to what you think, I have one or two tucked away for special occasions."

"I'm special?" She gazed up at him, a twinkle in her eyes. If she could tease, so could he.

"Probably. But so is the charity event." He grinned, reaching out to pet Bella. "Nice dog handbag. Clashes a little, but it's all for a good cause." She licked his hand excitedly, happy to be noticed.

Damien took Lissa's hand and led her toward the jeep.

"We could take my car tonight." Lissa offered.

"We could. But only if you let me drive."

She stopped short, a slight frown on her face. "*Hmmm*. I've seen you drive. The Jeep it is."

He opened the door and watched as Lissa attempted to climb in but failed miserably with the dress wrapped tightly around her legs and not much wiggle room.

"On second thought, let's take the Porsche. I don't want to split my dress and expose parts that will make tomorrow's headlines."

Damien grinned. "Sounds good to me. Driving the Porsche," he added when she shot him a surprised look.

"Oh, okay." She laughed. "For a minute there, I thought—"

"Hardly."

"Good." She tossed him the keys, and they headed for the garage. "See that we get there in one piece. Me and the car," she teased, a light laugh reaching his ears.

"Before I forget, Johnny Miller called to update me on Jasper. The guys got a long record. Turns out taking the other dogs was part of a diversionary tactic to instill fear in you before he carried out the ransom plan. He wanted to make you suffer."

"It worked. But at least it brought you back into my life."

"It did at that. And while we have a few minutes, I think we should talk. About us. About what's been going on between us."

"I'm listening." She turned to face him, but he kept his eyes on the road. *Mostly*. Glancing her way occasionally, he couldn't help but enjoy the relaxed closeness they shared. Days ago, he hadn't thought it possible.

"First off, I want you to know I would never say anything to hurt you. Ever."

"What did Bev say to you?"

"She told me what Haley said to you, and what you think you heard the other night at the party."

"Don't worry about it. It's not a big deal." The tension in her voice and the way she held herself stiff and unyielding said it was a big deal.

"I disagree. Anything Haley claimed I said was a lie. And the other night, I'm sorry you overheard what those catty women said, but you should know the only thing I'm guilty of is turning the table on them and defending you."

"But they were laughing."

"At Margie and what I said. Not at you."

"What did you say?"

Damien smiled, remembering the look of shock on Margie's face. "I told her I was sorry her husband lost out in the race, but to cut him and you some slack. And that it wasn't your fault if a man got distracted by a female driver's rear...bumper."

Lissa's laughter filled the car. "You didn't?"

"I did."

"You're incorrigible."

"I'll take that as a compliment. Here's the second and more important part. I want you to know as far as I'm concerned, there is an us. We've had nine years to figure this out. Long enough for even the slowest of men to realize he made a mistake and want to change the ending."

Lissa's hand touched his shoulder before sliding to the back of his neck, her warmth distracting, but nice. More than nice.

"That certainly makes things easy, because I agree." Lissa's words were the confirmation he needed.

Damien relaxed. "When did you change your mind?"

"Somewhere in between last night's collision and your kiss." Her fingers massaged the back of his neck. It reminded him of his poor choice of location for this conversation. His focus was torn between driving and the warmth of her skin against his.

"Last night was a wake-up call for me. You don't have to retire, you know. It won't change anything between us if you decide to keep racing. Nothing's official yet. It's a part of you, and I can accept that, just like I can accept your very public image."

"Wow. Quite a change of heart."

"Well, you're quite a woman. Besides, I've watched you in action enough to know you can handle just about anything the media throws your way. If you don't mind, why should I?"

"I can't believe I'm hearing this coming from you. As to retiring, my decision stands. It's time. Don't get me wrong, I love racing. But there are more important things I want to do with my life."

"Like the rescue shelter?" Damien knew she was passionate about the shelter, and it made sense. It was one of the things he loved about her. She was the most caring and compassionate woman he'd ever met.

"Like the rescue shelter," she repeated. "And spend time with you."

"I like the sound of that." He reached for her hand and gave it a squeeze, wishing for the tenth time they were somewhere else so he could kiss her again.

"Hands on the wheel, mister." Lissa laughed.

"I was wondering how long it would take you to comment on my driving." He grinned but did as she said. There was no denying the power under the hood or the exhilaration that came with driving the car, but her need for control was very much like his own. Something that could make the future interesting if tonight went well.

He pulled up to the Windsor hotel and parked in the valet lane. Everywhere he looked, people were dressed to the nines and headed inside. They made their way toward the ballroom.

"Over here. There's someone I want you to meet." She pulled his arm and led him across the lobby toward the buxom woman waving at her.

"Ruby! You made it." Lissa hugged the brunette, her affection genuine.

"Lissa! Congratulations on yesterday's win. I wish I'd been there to see it." Ruby gave Bella a kiss, petting her behind her ears. The dog knew how to milk the attention and turned her head to the side for a better angle.

"It was amazing. Thank you." Lissa was radiant as she recounted the final moments of the race.

"Who's your friend?" The woman turned her attention on him, curiosity in her gaze.

"Oh, sorry. This is Damien Trent, a special friend of mine." Lissa took his arm and pulled him close.

"Special, huh? Anyone with eyes can see that. Tell me something I don't know." Ruby grinned.

"Damien, this is Ruby Ross. I've known her since college, although we didn't really get to know each other until a few years ago. She's an incredible fashion designer. The dress I'm wearing is one of her designs. She does a lot of fashion layouts for *Bloom*, the same magazine I was doing the fragrance photoshoot for the other day. We reconnected at one of the parties and have been friends ever since."

"Lovely to meet you. I've been admiring your handiwork since I picked Lissa up this evening. Nice dress." He shook hands with Ruby, surprised to find himself pulled in for a hug.

Ruby laughed. "Thank you. You've got yourself a handful with this guy. Ever the flatterer."

"Where's that new husband of yours?" Lissa asked.

"Brandon's around here somewhere. I sent him to find us some champagne." Ruby searched the room and pointed over to the bar in the corner. "There he is. Attracting women as usual, but I don't worry. He knows a good thing when he's got it." She winked.

"That's great. I'm so glad you could come tonight."

"Of course. It's for a great cause, and I get to see you."

Lissa turned to Damien. "Ruby also has a corgi.

By the way, where is Diamond?"

"Up in the room. I'll check on her a little later. The flight here didn't seem to agree with the little diva, so she's resting."

"Good idea." Lissa smiled. "I've got to get inside and make the rounds. I'm sure we'll get a chance to talk again."

"You can count on it. It was nice to meet you, Damien."

"It was my pleasure." Damien escorted Lissa into the ballroom, leaving her side only long enough to secure her a fresh glass of wine when needed. He watched from the bar as Prince Dorian approached her, the two hugging and then chatting like old friends. Not for the first time, Damien wished the guy would head back to Avingdale, or Avington, or wherever it was he hailed from.

Much to Damien's satisfaction, by the time he got the drinks, the prince and his bodyguards had moved on and Lissa was talking with someone new. She was outgoing and everyone loved her. According to Bev, Lissa liked her privacy, but none of what he saw tonight backed up that theory.

By the time the music started, Damien was more than ready to put his plan into action. He took her by the hand and faced her. "Lissa, we seemed to have missed our first dance. Now's my chance to make it up to you. Would you care to dance?"

"I thought you'd never ask." She placed her hand in his, and he led her to the dance floor.

Damien pulled her in close, inhaling the now-familiar cinnamon and citrus fragrance that teased his senses with every move she made. *La Bella*. Lissa's signature fragrance was a scent he would never grow tired of. They waltzed around the dance floor, keeping perfect time to the strains of "Unforgettable." It was as if Nat King Cole had written the song with Lissa in mind.

The song ended, and the moment was upon Damien. It was time to take a leap of faith and find out if Lissa felt the same way he did. He reached into his pocket and pulled out the black box he'd stowed there earlier.

Dropping to one knee, Lissa stared down at him, her eyes wide with shock. But it was the slow smile that lit up her face that gave him the confidence to continue. All around him, people stopped to watch. Even the band stopped playing.

"Lissa Walker, queen of the racetrack and queen of my heart, will you do me the honor of becoming my wife? I love you with all that I am and will be yours forever and ever if you say yes."

She nodded, tears rolling down her face. "I can't believe this. Yes, of course. I love you, too."

Damien stood, slid the ring on her finger, and pulled her into his embrace.

"It's beautiful." She gazed down at her hand. "How on earth did you manage to get a ring by tonight?"

"It was my grandmother's." Damien kissed the back of her hand.

"It's lovely. That's the sweetest and most perfect ring you could have chosen."

The crowd cheered, offering well wishes throughout the night. Bev and Ruby took turns taking care of Bella, letting Damien dance with his fiancée. He still couldn't believe she'd said yes.

The evening drew to a close, and Lissa stepped up to the podium. "I want to thank you all for coming. Tonight has been a huge success thanks to each and every one of you. Between the ticket sales and your generosity, I am pleased to announce we have already raised five hundred and forty-eight thousand dollars. More than enough to build the rescue shelter." A round of applause reverberated across the room. Damien was proud of Lissa and all that she'd accomplished. She was making a difference in the world, and it made him love her even more if it were possible.

"In addition, your well-wishes tonight for my more recent personal development have left me moved in a way I will always remember. As most of you know, I announced my retirement from racing last night, but you all are the first to know why. I've decided to dedicate my time and energy as the new manager and spokesperson for our local rescue shelters. I want to do more than an annual charity event. I want to forward the cause year-round. And it's my promise to you, Charlotte will have the best rescue shelters possible. My goal is to branch out to other areas of the country eventually, and not just by giving money, but by giving them the manpower they need. Our canine and feline friends need us as much as we need them. Thank you again for your support and your generosity."

Cheers erupted again as Lissa stepped off the stage.

"You're a natural up there." Damien hugged her.

"I wouldn't go that far, but I'm working on it. It's easier when I'm dealing with something I care very much about. Easier still with you by my side."

"Always and forever." Damien pulled her close, unable to believe such an amazing woman had just agreed to marry him.

"Do you mind if I take your picture?" A photographer had joined them. Asking first was a nice change.

Lissa looked at him, the question in her eyes clearly telling him it was his decision.

He knew the pictures would be in every major newspaper tomorrow morning. But for once, Damien didn't care. Lissa was all that mattered. He took her in his arms, leaned her back, and kissed her in a way no one would mistake the love in his heart. And then he shot a grin at the cameraman. "How's that for an answer Mrs. Soon-To-Be-Trent?"

"Perfect." Lissa reached for Bella, and the three of them posed for one last shot. One big happy family.

If you enjoyed this sweet and charming romance, be sure to check out the ALSO BY ELSIE DAVIS section on the next page for more clean and wholesome romance.

BONUS READ

Want to keep in touch with new releases and what's happening in the world of Elsie Davis? Sign up for the monthly newsletter at Elsie Davis HEA (Happily-Ever-After) and enjoy DIGGING THE DRIVER (A Celebrity Corgi Romance) as a FREE BOOK!
The greatest compliment you could give an author is to leave a review in order to help other readers discover the same great stories you enjoyed. Amazon/Bookbub/Goodreads are all great places. Many thanks!!!
Another great way to keep in touch - *Follow Elsie Davis on FaceBook*

Also By Elsie Davis

Sweet, Clean and Wholesome Stories...with a Happily-Ever-After Guarantee!

Holidays in Hallbrook
(Sweet Romance Series for Holidays Throughout the Year)
Welcome to Hallbrook, New Hampshire. A small-town filled with the unexpected, lots of love, and of course, a beloved dog to ramp up the excitement.
Love & Order (Labor Day)
Love & Family (Thanksgiving)
Love & Peace (Christmas)
Love & Chocolate (Valentine's Day)
Love & Hope (Mother's Day)
Love & Liberty (Independence Day)

Love & Honor (Veteran's Day)
Love & Joy (Easter)
Love & Adventure (Father's Day)

Great Smoky Mountain Getaways
(Christian Inspirational – Women's Fiction Romances)
Juliet's Journey to Love
Poppy's Path to Love
Rachel's Road to Love

Crossroads Creek Cowboys
(Christian Inspirational Romances)
The Heart of a Cowboy
The Help of a Cowboy
The Return of a Cowboy
Coming Soon – The Care of a Cowboy

Crestfield Inn Romances
If you like special kinds of soulmates, a splash
of the supernatural, and wholesome relation-

ships, you'll adore this sweet bit of fun filled
with romance and mystery.
Turning Back Time
Turning Up Roses
Turning Down Pie

Celebrity Corgi Romance
(Standalone Sweet Romance)
If you like light mystery mixed in with
your happily-ever-after, you'll enjoy this sec-
ond-chance romance and the race to save an
adorable Corgi.
Digging the Driver

Gold Coast Retrievers
(Sweet Romance)
**Special Golden Retrievers help their humans
solve mysteries, save lives, and even find love...**
Defending Dakota

Trinity River

(Sweet Western Romance)
Ranchers and farmers depend on the Trinity River for water, but when a secret conglomerate starts buying up property by fair means or foul, it's time for the landowners of Tumble County to fight back—Texas style. But what they don't count on, is finding love in the process.
Back in the Rancher's Arms
Small Town, Big Secrets

Coming Soon! (2023-2024)

Sundancer's Legacy – 9 Book series

Sundancer's Star
Sundancer's Joy
Sundancer's Heart
Sundancer's Majesty
Sundancer's Miracle
Sundancer's Glory
Sundancer's Kiss
Sundancer's Moon

Sundancer's Splendor

About The Author

Elsie Davis is a *USA Today and International Bestselling Author* of over 25 sweet, clean, and wholesome romances, and a member of the ACFW. She discovered the world of Happily-Ever-After romance at the age of twelve when she began avidly reading Barbara Cartland, the Queen of Romance, and has been hooked ever since. After building her dream log home on top of a small mountain, she turned her attention to do what she loves most, writing. Elsie writes sweet Contemporary Romance and Contemporary Christian Romance from her heart...hoping to share a little love in a big world.

When she's not writing, she can be found birding, kayaking, camping, fishing, playing disc golf, and taking nature walks—hoping to

spot wildlife. Basically, she loves all things out-
doors, EXCEPT cold weather. She and her husband are avid Caribbean cruisers, but Elsie's
favorite vacation was their cruise to Alaska. (In
spite of the cold!) Indoors, she enjoys a toasty
fire, and of course, a great romance with a guaranteed Happily-Ever-After.

https://www.elsiedavishea.com

www.ingramcontent.com/pod-product-compliance
Lightning Source LLC
Chambersburg PA
CBHW020059310726
48970CB00002B/397

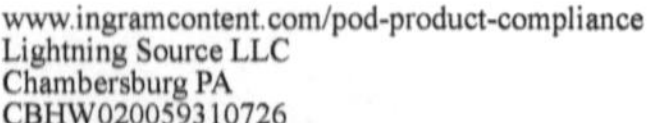